THE
GIRL
WHO
RUINED
CHRISTMAS

THE
GIRL
WHO
RUINED
CHRISTMAS

A TWEEN HOLIDAY NOVELLA

CINDY
CALLAGHAN

SPARKPRESS

Published by SparkPress, a BookSparks imprint,
A division of SparkPoint Studio, LLC
Phoenix, Arizona, USA, 85007
www.gosparkpress.com

Published 2021
Printed in the United States of America
Print ISBN: 978-1-68463-115-5
E-ISBN: 978-1-68463-116-2

Library of Congress Control Number: 2021910250

Interior design by Tabitha Lahr

DEDICATION

This book is dedicated to the many people who've shaped some of my most wonderful holiday memories. To name them all would be impossible, but here are a few standouts:

Mom, who bought the red and green paper for paper chains, and then more paper for more paper chains, and more paper . . .

Kevin, who took me to cut down my first tree.

Happy, for "Thank you, dear Santa" in response to a Hannah Montana microphone, a phrase that now lives in infamy.

Evan, who nearly got coal one year . . . it was too close to be funny.

Ellie, who gleefully opened tickets to "Jaquille and Hydett."

Finn, who for one month loves nothing more than sleeping under the tree, and **Bergen,** who cherished a month of batting ornaments off the bottom limbs.

Grandma, who let me put my thumbprint in the dough of her thumbprint cookies.

PopPop, who risked his life to hold the pinata way overhead so we kids could whack it every year.

Rache, who taught me about the Feast of the Seven Fishes.

Chris, with whom I celebrated that lesser-known holiday of Christmas Eve Eve.

Traci, whose birthday is the 26th and adored our rendition of Happy Birthday, which was purposely sung as badly as we could muster . . . I mean, *baaaaad.*

Don, who cut intricate paper snowflakes to tape on the red wall in their basement.

Aunt Vene and Uncle Roy, who hid Mom's gift of a puppy (Gyzmo) until the big day.

Aunt Helga, who always, without fail, got me "that one last present" that I opened late Christmas afternoon.

Joe and Missy, who hid the Yeti cooler, among other things, from Kevin.

Mel and Jen, with whom Ellie and I were stranded in NYC during a snowstorm that crippled all transportation.

Marini's Produce Stand, who make the holidays special for our whole community with their Christmas trees and gorgeous handmade decorations, and in many ways inspired the fictitious Schneider's Tree Farm in this book.

Dad, who read aloud in front of the fireplace, and all parents who read aloud to their children. And to Theodore Geisel for *The Grinch* and Clement C. Moore for *'Twas the Night Before Christmas.*

And to all readers, wishing you and yours a happy and safe holiday season.

CHAPTER 1

If you search for images of "teen locked in Harper Hollow Falls jail," you'd see a picture of thirteen-year-old Brady Bancroft in soaked Chuck Taylors and frozen Hello Kitty socks. The expression on her face would say, "This whole town hates me."

That girl would be me.

I'm Brady Bancroft.

CHAPTER 2

A week earlier: November 27

Me and my best friend Lou Lou sip bubble tea and scope out the best place to plant ourselves on the beach.

"Here?" I ask and point to a spot near a group of sandcastle builders.

Lou Lou faces toward the sun as if "trying on" this spot, because it might somehow feel different than another spot. "Yup. Good." She spreads her blanket and notices me eying the struggling castle sculptors.

I ask her, "Should I?"

"They do look like they need you."

I drop my beach bag and hand Lou Lou my tea. I approach the castle makers and offer, "I could give you a hand . . ."

When the man nods I help myself to a nearby icing spatula, and in a few flicks of my wrist I've smoothed and rounded the turret perfectly into shape.

I accept his thanks and return to my towel and tea.

Lou says, "You're like a superhero."

Taking my position to bask in the warm southern California sun, I brag, "One of my many talents."

Before closing my eyes to catch a snooze so that my vocal cords will be well rested for a cappella group practice later, I see Allie Moskowitz—Orange County Junior High's "it girl"—leave the Venice Beach sidewalk and head in our direction.

She's holding a remote-controlled gadget in one hand, while a second gadget flies overhead.

"Hi, Allie," I say.

"Hi, girls." She flashes her bright smile. As far as It Girls go, Allie is one of the good ones.

"What's that?" Lou asks.

"Oh my gosh, the latest. Isn't it amaze? It can take aerial pictures and send them right to my phone."

Lou asks, "Lemme see."

"Oh, I'm not taking pictures right now, silly. But I could, if I wanted to."

I ask, "What do you want to take pictures of?"

Allie sighs. "I'm not really into taking pictures."

Me and Lou Lou exchange a look of confusion.

"Then what's it for?" I ask.

Allie says, as if the answer is totally obvious, "To *have*."

My pause tells her that I don't understand.

"Just to have. You know what they say, the one who dies with the most toys wins."

I sort of nod. And notice Allie salivating over the sight of my purple-green drink a quarter of the way filled with popping boba.

"Don't even tell me that's the new lavender flavor."

"It is. Want to try?"

Allie takes the cup and sips. "Mmm. Best. Invention. Ever."

"Better than that?" I indicate her remote thing.

"Tough call. Luckily, we don't have to choose. We can have them both, right?" Then Allie says, "See you tonight at practice," and we watch her walk back toward the sidewalk.

"She took your drink," Lou Lou says.

"I know."

Lou Lou hands me her drink. "I woulda done the same thing."

I sip Lou's chocolate tea-based drink and set it between us in the sand.

Our eyes follow Allie as she walks along staring at her phone, drinking my drink, her hover camera over her head, oblivious that she's stepping on people's towels and into kids' sand projects.

"Is she horrible?" I ask.

"Only mildly." Lou tilts her head. "And not on purpose, I think."

"I'm so jelly of her," I confess.

"Me too," Lou says.

We share a laugh at how stupid it is to be jealous of Allie, and then Lou asks, "So, New York State?

"Yeah. Just two days. My dad has to meet some businesspeople. Me and Mom are tagging along. A little pre-Christmas fam time."

"I'm sure your posts will look fab, and Allie will be jelly of you."

"I'll do my best."

CHAPTER 3

he airport smells like a pine tree forest. There must
be twenty fresh trees. A group of children dressed
in matching elf outfits stand in three neat rows and
belt out "We Wish You a Merry Christmas." Overhead, a
man scales the wall in a safety harness, changing the date
on a giant calendar to November 28.

My dad collects our suitcases from the baggage car-
ousel while my mom paces around, hugging herself to
keep warm.

"I thought Christmas countdown calendars started
in December," I say, watching the Spiderman do his job.

"It gets pushed earlier every year," Mom says. "You
know they wanted to start the bazaar this weekend, but I
insisted they wait until I get back. I mean, after all, I *am*
the chairwoman this year."

In a few minutes, Dad has not only loaded a luggage cart but also obtained the keys to a rental car. He says, "All set," just in time to rescue me from Mom telling me again about the honor of being head of the Christmas bazaar.

The SUV is right out front of the airport. I sit in the car with the heat blasting and watch Dad load the luggage while Mom opens her bags to layer herself with sweater after sweater . . . adding a scarf, a coat, another scarf, and, finally, mittens and earmuffs.

She tries to get into the front seat, but she can't fit because she's bundled herself up so much. "Rob," she calls to my dad, who has added the address into the GPS. "A little help."

Dad comes around the car, moves Mom's seat all the way back and tilts it so that she's practically in my lap.

"Thanks, honey," she says as she lies in the passenger seat.

Not five minutes later, we pass a sign that says

HARPER HOLLOW FALLS, NEW YORK,
POPULATION 1,101.

"Tell me again why we're here?" I ask.

"This is your father's biggest deal ever, Brady. It could change his career." Mom takes off her earmuffs and one of the many scarves.

"I thought you already had a great career," I say. "Aren't you Mr. Real Estate?"

Mom answers for him (she always answers for him), "He is, but now he could be the King of Real Estate. Couldn't you, honey?" Before Dad can speak, she says, "He totally can." She unzips her coat and reaches for the temperature control, but she's too constrained by her outfit for her hand to reach the knob. "Rob, can you lower this a bit? It's stifling."

Dad turns the knob.

I point to the windshield, which is being splatted by tiny white particles falling from the sky. "What the heck?" The particles connect into bigger, fluffier white flakes. "I've never seen snow!"

"We're about as far north as New York goes, practically in Canada," she says. "Lots of snow here."

"Awesome. It's so pretty."

"Brady, maybe you don't truly understand snow," she says. "Why do you think so many people live in California?"

"I don't know how anyone could hate something so white and fluffy."

"You say that now." Then Mom adds, "But, don't worry, we'll be back in the Golden State in a few days for the Christmas bazaar. Being the chairwoman? Sure, it's a lot of work, but it's an honor, really. Are you going to help? We could use it. And maybe Lou Lou too?"

"I'll ask her," I say, but I know Lou Lou won't want to. Last year we helped out with the bazaar by setting up a row of twenty pink artificial Christmas trees in the school gym. They were aluminum and gave us little cuts on our hands.

Dad stops the rental SUV outside of the Yuletide Bed & Breakfast, a big stone Colonial house with a Christmas wreath already hung on every window.

I step out of the toasty car, look up, and open my mouth to let flakes in. "I love snow!"

Mom puts her earmuffs back on. "Come on. Let's go inside." She hustles to the front door and calls back to Dad, "Rob, can you get our bags, honey?"

I fling my backpack on my shoulder and follow.

The smell of chocolate chip cookies permeates the walls of the B&B and sails right up my nose. *Mmmmm.* Meanwhile, snowflakes accumulate into a dust-like layer on the ground and on the holly bushes that stand on either side of the front door.

Before Mom can knock, the door flies open.

"Come in. Come in. You must be the Bancrofts," says a short woman with rosy cheeks and a spotted apron. She holds the door open for my dad, who's struggling with our luggage.

"You need a hand with that?" asks a man in a neon-green tracksuit, walking vigorously up a driveway lined with lantern lights. His arms swing in synch with his giant strides, speed-walking style. "Let me." He takes a leather duffel bag off my dad's shoulder and a briefcase out of his hand. "I'm Kenny, Kenny Crispin. My wife Carmella and I own this here B&B. You've picked the best time of year to come to Harper Hollow Falls. We're all about Christmas. The mistletoe gets hung before Thanksgiving."

The woman, Carmella Crispin, closes the door behind us once Kenny, Dad, and the luggage are inside. She wraps her arms around herself, and excitedly says, "Oooo, it's starting to get cold."

"Dreadfully cold," Mom adds, less enthusiastically.

"I love it," Kenny says. "The colder, the better. That's what I say."

Mom finds the fireplace and positions her butt a few inches away from it without making it appear as though she's toasting her buns.

I look around the house. Kenny Crispin wasn't kidding about Christmas. We still had leftover Thanksgiving turkey in the fridge at home—I mean, it was two days ago—but the Crispins' tree is up and fully trimmed. White lights twinkle in every built-in bookshelf and nook of the B&B.

"Your decorations are great," I say. "I like this one." I indicate a countdown-to-Christmas figurine. Today it reads twenty-eight.

"Thank you, dear," Carmella Crispin says. "It might still be November, but I just get so excited, I can't stand it. My favorite thing to do every day is switch the number." Then she adds, "Maybe I'll let you do it tomorrow." She's visibly giddy with anticipation.

"That'd be cool," I say. "We don't have one of those."

"I can show you the most darling little shop where they make them." Then Carmella Crispin asks Mom and Dad, "What brings you to our little hollow?"

"Business," Mom says, indicating Dad.

"What kind of business you in?" Kenny Crispin asks Dad.

Mom answers for him. Dad knows Mom loves to talk, and since he doesn't, they're kind of a perfect couple. "He's in real estate. He's here to look at Schneider's Tree Farm for development."

The smiles instantly drain from Kenny and Carmella's rosy-cheeked faces. Either they have no idea what Mom is talking about, or they have every idea and don't like it. Mom adds, "For a factory."

Kenny says flatly, "We know."

"We've heard," Carmella says.

"The Schneiders are dear friends of ours." Kenny picks up the bags and turns to bring them up the curved staircase.

"Then they must've told you how good this will be for your town?" Mom asks. "Create jobs."

Carmella clears her throat. "Let's not talk about it." Then she straightens up, seeming to flip an internal switch that reignites the sparkle in her eyes. She faces me. "I'll show you to your room, and we can head out to see Ol' Sturdy Stan McSpruce."

"Who's that?" I ask.

"Ol' Sturdy isn't a 'who,' it's a 'what,'" Kenny Crispin explains from the bottom step with a festive giggle.

"The pride and joy of Harper Hallow Falls," Carmella adds. "Something very special is happening tonight in the town square, where Ol' Sturdy Stan stands."

"What?" I ask. "What's happening?"

"Now, you don't want me to spoil the surprise," Carmella says.

Kenny adds, "That would be like opening a present before Christmas."

CHAPTER 4

C armella and Kenny drive us to the town square in their pickup truck. Lots of snow has fallen in the last hour and continues dropping in big fluffy clumps.

Kenny Crispin parks a block away from the town square, where it looks like half of the population of Harper Hollow Falls is gathered.

When my Chuck Taylors hit the ground, a wet cold seeps through the canvas. A chill shoots through my whole body, and just then I start thinking that maybe Mom knows what she's talking about; snow is pretty, I mean really, really pretty, but *brrrr.*

"Here, dear." Carmella puts a hat on my head.

No ordinary hat, a stocking cap.

If I were to search images for "insanely embarrassing winter hat," the knitted, striped job that is now on my head would appear. I follow Carmella, and guess what? The cap's pom-pom swings against my lower back while I walk. Luckily, she didn't think to add jingle bells to it.

A crowd gathers around a massive evergreen tree in the center of town.

Kenny props his hands on his hips and stares at it with a broad smile that expresses something—pride. "That's Ol' Sturdy Stan McSpruce."

"The tree?" I ask.

Carmella explains, "It was planted here by the founders of Harper Hollow Falls to create a town center where everyone could gather and build a community."

"It's the heart of our special little northern oasis," Kenny adds.

Mom snuggles next to Dad to stay warm. "And why is everyone gathered out here tonight?"

At that question the sound of hooves vibrates off the snow.

Clop.

Clop.

Clop.

Kenny Crispin doesn't answer. Instead, he calls to a man, "Is that it?"

I can't imagine that the guy isn't freezing in only a red T-shirt over a turtleneck. Maybe his faded red baseball hat keeps his head warm, but not nearly as toasty as my fab colorful stocking cap. My head might *look* ridiculous, but it's warm—I wish I could say the same about my feet, which are probably pruney blocks of ice by now.

"Is that it?" Kenny asks him again.

"That's it! There she is!" the man in the red hat says.

Four Clydesdale horses pull an evergreen tree on a wagon toward the center of the crowd. The driver yanks on the reins and expertly parks the team.

The man in the red hat, who looks about Dad's age, now stands next to us and stares at the tree. "Isn't she a beaut?" I notice his feet are snug in wool socks that peek out the top of gold work boots thickly covered with mud.

"It's the most stunning tree I've ever seen," Carmella Crispin says, and then she whispers to Ol' Sturdy Stan McSpruce, "No offense. You're a classic; a treasure."

The man in red breaks eye contact with the wagon and kisses Carmella on the cheek, then pats Kenny on the back. Then he introduces himself to Mom and Dad with a handshake. "Daniel Schneider. If you come by the farm, I'll help you find the perfect tree. Any friends of the Crispins are friends of mine, so you get the ten-percent discount."

"He gives everyone a ten-percent discount," Carmella whispers to us.

Daniel Schneider asks, "What kind of folks are you? Fraser? Douglas fir? Blue spruce? Balsam?"

"They're from California," Kenny offers. "Los Angeles."

Schneider says, "Ah. That explains why I don't recognize you. I figured you were one of the few folks making the long trek down from Porter City, Canada, this year, what with the big news and all." Then to Kenny, he says, "Just wish it was easier for them to get here, *eh*?"

"Oh, yeah," Kenny and Carmella agree. "That'd be great for business."

"What news?" Mom asks.

"That tree," Carmella points to the one on the wagon, "has been selected for the White House."

"Seriously?" I ask.

"That's amazing," Mom says. "Congratulations. Where in the White House?"

"The East Wing entrance. We're very proud of it," Daniel Schneider says. "And the timing couldn't be more perfect. There's some stupid company that wants to build some stupid factory on my farm to make something stupid for stupid people to buy—"

"Uh, Dan—" Kenny says.

"Sneakers, I think. I mean, does the world need more stupid sneakers?"

"Dan—" Kenny tries again.

Schneider continues, "My farm has been in the family for three generations. And they might've been able to buy it right out from under me, on account of some back taxes that the government says we owe. But now, with this

White House hubbub, business is going to be massive. It would really boom if there was a bridge over the river for the folks from Porter City to easily get here. Then I'd be able to pay that tax bill and get Uncle Sam off my back for sure." He wipes his nose on his sleeve. "So, did you say you were Balsam people?"

"Kind of ironic," I say.

"What is?" Schneider asks me.

"That your government problem is being fixed by the government's tree selection," I say.

"Right." He looks at my dad. "Smart kid." Then to me, he says, "Nice hat. Looks good on you."

I don't think he actually thinks the hat is nice at all. "I'm thirteen," I say to correct his "kid" comment.

"Well, that explains it," Daniel Schneider says. "You look cold. Maybe you should get some hot cider over at the café . . . uh, what's your name, Thirteen-Year-Old?"

"Brady Bancroft."

"Bancroft . . . Bancroft . . . I know a Bancroft."

Kenny says, "Dan, this here is Rob Bancroft. From LA."

Carmella adds, "He's the *guy*—"

Mom interrupts. "The stupid guy, who works for the stupid company."

I whisper to Mom, "He didn't say the guy was stupid, just the company, the factory, the sneakers, and the people buying the sneakers."

Daniel Schneider turns his ball cap frontward. "I see. You aren't here to buy a tree, and you aren't here for our little bon voyage to send this bad boy to DC. So why *are* you here?" he asks Dad.

Mom answers for him. "To close the real estate deal before the holidays."

Daniel Schneider looks right at my dad, even though Mom was the one talking. "Well, like I said, there isn't going to be a deal on account of the White House news. It's what we here in this little town of Harper Hollow Falls call a 'game changer.' Seems you came all the way from your SoCal metropolis for nothing."

There's an awkward beat of silence, and then Daniel Schneider adds, "You may as well at least take advantage of the hot cider. It's the best in Two Pines County, and south-east-central Canada." He points to one of the storefronts on the square—Blitzen's Café. "In there." The windows are steamed up like it's warm and cozy inside. "Oh, and if you change your mind about getting a tree, the full price is marked on the tag."

Schneider turns his hat backward again, gives a quick see-you-later grin to Kenny and Carmella, and walks to the wagon.

I guess he doesn't give everyone a discount.

CHAPTER 5

"**N**ot exactly a warm welcome," Mom says. "But I guess it's no surprise that they're mad about the factory." To me she asks, "Do you want cider?"

"Yeah." I shiver. "Right after I get a picture of those Clydesdales for InstaPic."

"OK. We'll meet you inside," Mom says, and then she and Dad walk toward Blitzen's.

I am navigating through the crowd to the horses when my feet slide out from under me, and I'm just about to face-plant into the snow when I'm caught. The cap has fallen over my eyes. I push it up to find warm, ocean-blue eyes looking at me.

"You okay?" my savior asks. "That was close."

"Yeah . . . I'm okay. Thanks." Before I can ask his name, he's lost in a crowd focused on a tall, lanky woman with long brown hair standing on a podium. She holds a megaphone and plops a top hat on her head. "Hello, neighbors. It's time to say goodbye to our little gem—well, not so little. Am I right?" She laughs at herself with a snort.

She continues, "I always knew someone from Harper Hollow Falls would make it to Washington, DC, to meet the president of the United States. I'd hoped it would be one of our high school graduates, maybe the Grossman boy, am I right?" She slaps her leg and the crowd howls with laughter. She's like a stand-up comedian. I overhear people standing next to me refer to her as the mayor, and say that "She's always hysterical, don't you think?"

"But seriously, folks, this is an honor just the same. A special moment in our town's colorful history. Please join me in wishing our tree good luck." Then she calls out louder, "Good luck, tree. Represent Harper Hollow Falls well and make us proud."

Everyone shouts well wishes to the tree. The noise causes the horses to shake their manes, and I notice the boy with the blue eyes patting them to assure them that everything is fine.

This is all so cool. I *have to* post a pic to make Allie Moskowitz jelly of *me*.

I examine myself in the shot, slide the stocking cap off my head, and fix my hair. I make a super cute smile.

Click!

My flash goes off as I snap a selfie with the Clydesdales, the White House Christmas tree, and the cute guy in the background.

At the blink of the flash, one of the horses freaks! I mean, *freaks*!

He bucks, making another horse neigh loudly. Horses three and four swing their bushy manes. Then all four storm off with a thunderous *clop-clop*, pulling the wagon, its driver, and White House Christmas tree with the might of a runaway train.

The blue-eyed driver snaps the reins, struggling to get the wagon under control, but the horses make a sharp change of direction.

The driver is thrown off right before the wagon crashes into a telephone pole with enough oomph that the horses break loose, galloping away into the dark, snowy night.

The onlookers *oooh*.

Then they fall silent as the telephone pole knocks over a streetlight, which slowly falls onto the White House Christmas tree.

Everyone's mouths hangs open.

After a few dreadful moments, sparks jump from the telephone pole, the remaining streetlights go out, and Harper Hollow Falls' prize gem glows with amber flames.

All eyes go in the same direction, toward a girl.

That girl would be me: Brady Bancroft.

CHAPTER 6

T he fire department packs up its truck. No one has
been hurt, at least not physically.

I survey the damage: broken wagon, four missing
horses, telephone pole toppled onto a burnt tree, streetlight
through the front window of Blitzen's, no power, and the
water left by the fire company is quickly freezing.

Daniel Schneider sits on a curb with his red ball cap
folded in his hands. The whole town waits quietly for
him to say something. He only whispers, "What the heck
happened?"

That's when a girl in a fur-lined plaid bomber hat and
glasses points right at me. "It was her. The Canadian."

Someone else adds, "She used the flash on her phone
to spook the Clydesdales."

"Why did you do that?" Daniel Schneider asks me.
Then he squints in the dark, studying my face. "Wait.

You're not Canadian. You're the Bancroft girl. Did you think that destroying the White House tree would ruin my business and your father's stupid company could buy my farm?"

"Oh no. Nothing like that. I'm sorry. It was an accident. Really."

Everyone stares at me. If you were to search images for "Harper Hollow Falls's public enemy number one," you'd see a thumbnail of me in a striped stocking cap with a pompom.

"I swear. I didn't mean it. I only wanted a picture to show my friend."

The comedienne comes over, megaphone dangling at her side. "You might not want to say anything else." She isn't so funny now.

Mom runs to my side, Dad right behind her. "It was an accident."

"If your car crashes into a flock of Girl Scouts by accident, you're still responsible. This is no different." She adds, "Accidents have consequences."

"She's just a kid," Mom says.

The woman with the megaphone says, "In Harper Hollow Falls, destruction of property is a criminal matter."

"Oh, come on, a crime? Are you the police? Are you arresting her?" Mom asks.

"No, I'm not arresting her."

"Good. Phew. She didn't mean it, like she said. I'm glad we're all coming to our senses," Mom says.

A uniformed officer appears, and the woman with the megaphone says, "She'll arrest her." To the young officer she says, "Bring her in, Lily."

"What?!" Mom exclaims. "Brady, we'll get this all sorted. Don't worry about a thing."

The female officer touches my elbow. "This way."

I pull my arm away and explain. "It was an accident. I swear."

"Do I need to cuff you?"

"Cuff? No. Please, don't."

"Where are you taking her?" Mom asks. "Can they do this, Rob?"

For the first time since our arrival, my dad speaks. "Better not say anything, Brady."

CHAPTER 7

T he Crispins' pickup truck, with my mom and dad in the back seat, follows me in the police car.

I still have my phone. (I think the LA police probably would've taken it away.) I use it to search images for "Teen arrested for burning down would-be White House Christmas tree." Nothing. Yet.

We arrive at the Harper Hollow Falls police station, which is only a "station" in name. It's a stone house that looks a lot like the Yuletide Bed & Breakfast and is equally decked out for Christmas.

"Are you locking me up? Like, in a cell? Will there be other people there? Like, criminals?" I continue asking the officer questions. "Are they bank robbers? Con men?"

"I'm not at liberty to discuss ongoing investigations." I notice that her utility belt hangs low on her hips despite being tightened to the last hole. "But besides Mr. Burns not paying his parking tickets for five years, this is the biggest crime I've ever seen here. And I've lived in Harper Hollow Falls all my life."

The tag on her police jacket reads, "Officer Lily Morgan." Officer Lily, who seems too young and too small to be a cop, escorts me inside and quickly up a center staircase with a banister wrapped in a shimmery garland and white lights. It doesn't look like a staircase leading to prison.

"But, I mean, it's not really a crime. I was taking a selfie," I say.

"You destroyed someone else's property that just happened to be en route to the President of the United States. I'm not a lawyer, but that sounds like a crime to me. But, like I said, I'm not at liberty to discuss an ongoing investigation." Lily swipes a dangling piece of hair into the knot that sits low and tight on her neck.

"What do you think will happen to me?"

"That's up to the chief justice." She adds, "You're going to have to stop talking now."

"Chief justice? He sounds nice. Is he nice?" I ask.

"He's a 'she.' And she's as tough as they come. Now, stop talking. Anything you say can and will be used against you."

I ignore that last part. "Tough? What does that mean? Juvie? Maximum security? Labor camp? Will I get a parole officer? Is there a warden?"

"You know, 'tough.'" Lily adds, "But she's funny, too."

"Funny is good. Right?"

Lily doesn't answer because, apparently, we've arrived. She stops at a door on which hangs a countdown-to-Christmas sign: 28 DAYS. Lily changes the number to twenty-seven, fishes a keychain out of a pocket, and fiddles until she finds a brass skeleton key. She unlocks the door.

The walls are painted baby blue, the hardwood floors look recently polished, and there are wooden blinds on the window. That's where the interior decorating ends. On one side of the room are a cot and metal nightstand, and on the other side is a folding chair. There's enough space left in the room for a five-person yoga class. Not so much as a sprig of holly has made it into this room. I want to ask officer Lily for dry socks, but something about that request feels inappropriate—maybe it's the handcuffs hanging from her belt.

"I'll get you when the chief justice is ready," Lily says. "I wouldn't try to slide down the drainpipe for an escape. The last time Mr. Burns tried to do that, it pulled away from the house and he broke both his legs. He had to finish his sentence in hip-to-toe casts, and then pay for the repairs on top of his parking tickets and fines."

"Good to know." I rub my wrists and sit on the edge of the cot.

I hear Lily lock the door behind herself.

❄ ❄ ❄

And so . . . that's how I find myself locked in the Harper Hollow Falls jail: cold, wet, and hated.

I wrap the cot blanket around myself.

Mom said not to worry.

She'll call a lawyer, right?

Everything will be OK, right?

❄ ❄ ❄

I scan through my social media notifications on my phone. The news is out. Accompanying every angry emoji you can think of, some I'd never even seen before, were posts:

Brady Bancroft locked in Harper Hollow Falls jail . . .

13-year-old girl destroys town's Christmas . . .

What kind of person does that?

Grinch!

Scrooge!

To my phone I yell, "It was an *accident!*" The battery light blinks, so I turn the phone off. Images flash in my head:

- An image of me in front of a huge courtroom, sitting on a witness bench, while a crotchety old lawyer yells questions at me until I cry.
- One of me standing in the town center while everyone throws rotten tomatoes at me.
- Another of me and the guy with the parking tickets, Mr. Burns, playing cards in the prison yard.
- A series of time-lapse pictures of me looking out this window—first I'm thirteen, then in my thirties, then I'm gray and hunched over. *Will they give me a cane?*
- Finally, some Christmas Eve sixty years in the future, I'm released in a wheelchair, which they take away from me once I'm on a bus headed to California.

❄ ❄ ❄

Finally, Lily returns. It feels like it's been days, but it's only been forty-five minutes.

She has changed into a sweater embroidered with a picture of Santa sneaking a cookie, a denim mini skirt, snowflake tights, and cowboy boots. Her hair is out of its knot and flowing down to her waist. In her officer voice she says, "Let's go."

"You look nice," I say.

"I have a date, if you must know," Lily says. "And I can't engage in casual conversation with suspected criminals." She relocks handcuffs around my wrists.

"Who's it with?"

"Jamaal Walsh. Second date. Now stop talking."

"Do you like him?"

Lily breaks from her officer character and smirks. "I guess I do." She pauses, and I think that's all she's going to say, but she adds under her breath, "He sent me flowers the other day," then nudges me forward. "Remember you have the right to remain silent."

I walk toward the stairway we came up. Something's different. It's the smell. Someone's baking. I'm guessing it's Carmella Crispin, since it smells like the Yuletide. I ask Lily, "What are you and Jamaal going to do? And where are you taking me?"

"We're line dancing. He's a good dancer," Lily says. "You're going to see the chief justice."

"Dinner, too?" Then I ask, "What will happen with the chief justice?"

"Italian," Lily says. "She'll review your case." Then she adds, "Or maybe we'll just grab a burger."

We reach the bottom of the stairs. I was too distracted to look around when she brought me in, so now I check the place out. When this was used as a home, the rooms on either side of me were probably the dining room and the living room. One is refurbed like the reception area of a police station: a counter with stools, a computer, corkboards on the walls, and cubbies for officers to hang their coats and hats.

I hear my mom before I see her. "Rob, what did the lawyer say? Is he on the way?" Then she sobs. "I mean this whole thing is crazy, isn't it?" Another sob. "I can't believe this is happening."

Then I look into the former living room that is set up like a little courtroom: a leather chair sits behind a barn-wood table on which rest a gavel and a Bible. There's a row of dining room chairs against the wall where Mom, Dad, Kenny Crispin, and Daniel Schneider sit. Standing in the back with other townspeople are the cute boy with the blue eyes who drove the sleigh, the girl with the glasses and fur-lined hat who pointed me out to the crowd (*"It was her!"*), and another girl with a major resting Grinch face and turtleneck with the Schneider's Tree Farm logo.

Dad's talking into his cell phone.

Mom lets out a wail when she sees me in handcuffs.

Carmella Crispin walks up behind Lily and me with a plate of warm cookies.

"Before we start, a little treat." She holds the plate out for Lily, who takes one.

I shrug my shoulders, showing Carmella that I'm handcuffed.

"Oh, come on, Lillian Marie Morgan, can we take the drama down a notch? Handcuffs, really?"

Lily puts the cookie in her mouth to free her hands and unlocks my cuffs. When the cookie's out, she says, "Yes, Mrs. Crispin."

I bite into one. "Mmmm." That makes Mrs. Crispin smile with satisfaction as she delivers one to everyone else.

"Everything is better with a warm cookie," she says.

When Mom reaches for one, a megaphone blares, "All rise!" causing her to jump in her seat and drop the cookie.

Dad disconnects his cell.

Behind the megaphone walks the comedienne mayor from the send-off celebration, wearing a choir robe. She speaks into the megaphone, which is totally unnecessary in such a small room. She says, "All rise for the Honorable Chief Justice Winter of Harper Hollow Falls." Then she walks behind the table and takes the big leather chair. Once she's comfortable, she motions for everyone else to sit.

"*You're* the chief justice?" I ask.

She smiles broadly, picks up the megaphone, and uses it to bellow, "Yes." She sets it down, then picks it up again. "And the mayor."

CHAPTER 8

"Court is in session," states Chief Justice Winter. "We're here to review the charges against Miss Brady Evelyn Bancroft, age thirteen, from Los Angeles, California. They are destruction of property; cruelty to animals; intent to defile a cherished holiday fixture, in this case the town's sacred tree bound for the White House; intent to sabotage a business, in this case Blitzen's Café—home of the world's best hot cider; and criminal mischief. How do you plead?"

Mom blows her nose and dabs her eyes. When I glance over to her, I see Carmella hand her a cookie.

I say, "I didn't do any of that."

"You didn't maliciously flash a bright light in an innocent horse's eyes, causing him and his barn-mates to flee in fear and run into a telephone pole"—she looks at something on her cell phone—"all of the aforementioned horses, I may add, as of this moment, remain at large."

"Not *maliciously*," I offer.

"But these events were all set into motion as a direct result of your actions. Were they not?"

"Yes, but it was an accident."

"Let the record show that Miss B—" she looks around. "Who's taking the official record?"

No one is writing anything down.

The chief justice says, "Lily, please take a seat and write stuff down."

Lily looks at her watch. "You see, I have a . . . a . . . a . . . commitment."

The chief justice stares at her, stone-faced, no comedienne here.

Lily adds, "It's . . . um . . . of a personal nature."

The chief justice doesn't break eye contact, and Lily doesn't move to take notes. It's a real stare-down, one that Lily loses the second she looks at the floor.

To help Lily out (after all, we're practically gal pals), I whisper to the chief justice, "It's a date."

The judge's face lights up. She puts her elbows on the table and leans her face into her hands and asks Lily, "With whom? Oh, I bet it's that Choudhury boy. Isn't it?"

Lily doesn't say anything, so I say, "No."

"Klaus from the exterminating company?"

"No," I answer.

"Philip Grossman with the buck teeth?" The justice juts out her front teeth.

"No," I answer again.

"Hmmm," the judge thinks. "Oh, I know—"

"Judge!" Daniel Schneider interrupts.

The chief justice glares at him with a look that I wouldn't want to be on the receiving end of. She picks up the megaphone, and snaps at him, "Order in the court!"

"I apologize, Your Honor," he says cowering. "But, you know, the tree, the reason we're here . . ."

The chief justice doesn't respond to Daniel. Instead, she smiles at Lily. "You go on now. Have fun."

Lily begins to leave, but the chief justice calls to her, "Oh, and—" she mouths the words *call me*, while putting her thumb to her ear and her pinky to her mouth. Then she asks us, "Where were we?"

Daniel says, "She just confessed to everything. This is an open-and-shut case."

"But the official record." The chief justice calls to the reception area. "Mrs. Knox, are you out there?"

No one stirs. For a second, I focus on Mrs. Crispin, or really, on her cookies. I want another one. At this point, I haven't eaten in hours.

"Mrs. Knox!"

My stomach growls, thinking of cookies.

"Mrs. Knox!!"

A woman who's clearly over a hundred years old, and under four foot ten, shuffles in with the help of a walker sliding on tennis balls. She lifts her neck, which is hooked like a candy cane, to look up at the judge. "Yes, dear."

"Can you come in and take notes for me?"

"Sure. Just let me get paper." She begins shuffling out painfully slowly, when Daniel Schneider says, "You sit down, Mrs. Knox. I'll get it." He dashes out and back. Then he gets Mrs. Knox a chair next to the chief justice.

"Ready?" the chief justice asks her.

"What's that? I can't hear you, sweetheart."

Daniel Schneider drops his face into his hands and lets out a frustrated sigh. I can't blame him. I'm dying for dry shoes and maybe some soup.

Ahhh, soup. . . . *Does Mrs. Crispin make soup as good as she does cookies?*

"Are you ready?" the judge repeats to Mrs. Knox, much more loudly.

"Oh dear, no. I still have shopping and wrapping and baking and decorating to do. You know my motto: If it wasn't for the last minute, nothing would ever get done."

Carmella chuckles. Under normal circumstances, I might also, but I'm still plagued with the idea that I'll experience my teens, middle age, and golden years locked in a robin's-egg-blue bedroom in Harper Hollow Falls, New York.

The judge whispers to Mrs. Knox for a bit, and then Mrs. Knox readies herself to write things down.

Finally, the chief justice turns to me. "How do you plead?"

"Not guilty," I say.

"Ha!" Mrs. Knox laughs to herself as she writes. "That's not what I heard!"

"Why don't you tell me what happened," the judge says. *Finally!*

"The horses and tree were so pretty, and I was so excited about the whole White House thing. I mean, that's amazing—*the* White House! I wanted a picture to show my friend Lou Lou from California. So, I took off the stocking cap that Mrs. Crispin gave to me to wear and—"

"Oh, I love Carmella's hats almost as much as her cookies," Mrs. Knox mumbles to herself as she jots notes.

I continue, "And I took a selfie—"

"That's one of those phone pictures," Mrs. Knox explains to the chief justice.

I ignore her. "But it was dark—"

Daniel Schneider stands and points at me. "So, you used your flash and scared the Clydesdales. You set the whole fiasco into motion so that I wouldn't get the publicity for the White House tree and I wouldn't be able to pay the taxes and your dad's company could take my farm!"

Mrs. Knox exclaims, "Case dismissed!"

The chief justice smashes the gavel on the table. "Order!" Then she says, "Carmela. More cookies. For everyone. Now!"

Mrs. Crispin calmly delivers cookies. I take two because I'm so hungry.

Once things are quiet, I say. "I'm really sorry. I didn't mean it."

"A likely story," Mrs. Knox whispers, but not in a whispering way. "How can you believe someone who takes two cookies?" She focuses on her paper and taking notes.

I squint to see if she's written "two cookies" in the official record. Instead, I see a snowman! She's doodling a snowman!

"I'm ready to make my judgment," the chief justice says.

"That's all?" Mom asks. "What about character witnesses? Cross examination? Objections? Jury deliberations?"

"It won't change my mind, Mrs. Bancroft."

"But—"

The chief justice smacks the gavel again, and Mrs. Crispin shoves a cookie in my mom's mouth.

"Brady Bancroft, I hereby find you guilty."

CHAPTER 9

*G*uilty?"
My mom lets out a sigh.
Daniel Schneider claps.

Carmella Crispin dabs a tear with a cookie, then stuffs it in her mouth.

Dad asks, "What does that mean? Will she have a record?"

Bam! The chief justice smacks the gavel.

"Calm down. Order!" the chief justice cries.

"Justice is served," Mrs. Knox says.

Mom's sobs grow louder. "My baby is going to jail?"

Bam! Again with the gavel.

"Please," the judge says. "Let me explain the sentencing."

Everyone listens carefully.

"There will be no prison time, and no record, if Brady completes a month of community service to the court's satisfaction."

"See," Dad says to my mom. "She can do a community project at home, and we can put this all behind us."

"The community service will be conducted here in Harper Hallow Falls starting tomorrow, November twenty-ninth, and ending on December twenty-third. If at that time she has completed her sentence without incident, she will be released."

"But—" Mom starts.

"What about—" Dad starts.

"How will—" Kenny Crispin asks.

"Where will—" Daniel Schneider begins.

Bam!

Everyone quiets.

"Brady will conduct her service under the supervision of Mr. Schneider as an unpaid employee of his Christmas tree farm and perform the same way the other employees do. She will reside at the Yuletide Bed and Breakfast." To the Crispins, she asks, "That bedroom with the red gingham plaid curtains is available until the holidays, isn't it?"

They nod.

"Good. Mr. and Mrs. Bancroft, you may return home, assuming the Crispins are willing to serve as Brady's guardians." She asks the Crispins, "Are you?"

They nod.

"Good," the chief justice says.

"Go home without her?" Mom asks.

"Or you can stay in town, if you'd like. I just assumed you had busy lives to get back to in the city. You know, real estate empires to build . . ."

"I don't know about that, Rob."

"But, keep in mind, if you decide to stay, that she will be either working at the Christmas tree farm or residing at the Inn. There will be no frolicking to the mall, hair cutteries, or dinners out. Brady is basically under house arrest unless exceptions are made by Mr. Schneider or the Crispins. Am I clear?"

Dad pats Mom's arm and nods to the chief justice that they understand.

She asks me, "Do you understand, Miss Bancroft?"

"Yes."

Bam!

"Court is adjourned." To Mrs. Knox, the judge says, "Thank you for your service." She walks out from behind the table and out the front door, grabbing two cookies off of Carmela Crispin's plate on her way.

Daniel Schneider says to me, "I'll see you at nine a.m. sharp tomorrow. Dress warm." And he too leaves. The girl in the fur-lined hat and her friend trail after him, giving me glares. The cute boy follows them, but his look in my direction isn't nearly as cold.

Kenny sighs. "Well, it might not have been the verdict that you wanted. But it could have been much worse. She was in a good mood."

"That was a *good* mood?" Mom asks.

"Sometimes she can get grouchy," Carmella Crispin says. "Let's head back to the inn, and we can sort out the details."

CHAPTER 10

We gather around a fireplace at the Yuletide Bed & Breakfast. I am warm again, after a hot shower. Carmella sets out a tray of pigs in a blanket and a fresh pan of chocolate chip cookies.

Before she sits, she wraps an afghan around me, and then another around my mom. Since my grandparents aren't living, I decide to adopt the Crispins as my grandparents.

"Maybe while you're here, I can teach you to crochet," she suggests, offering me a plate with a pool of ketchup for dipping my mini hot dog wrapped in flaky, buttery crescent roll.

I'm not sure I love the idea of sewing, but at least it would be indoors, warm, and, I assume, accompanied by baked goods.

Mom says, "Thank you so much for agreeing to let Brady and I stay here. Rob will have to go home for work."

"Oh, it's no problem at all. Our five rug rats are all grown up, and I miss having someone to spoil," Carmella says.

Kenny adds, "We've done this sort of thing before."

"Oh?" Mom asks. "Does the chief justice give this type of sentence often?"

"Let's just say she doesn't take kindly to strangers disrespecting Harper Hollow Falls. And, if they step out of line, she likes to teach them a lesson rather than really get them in any legal trouble. But this is the most serious case I've ever seen."

"And the longest," Carmella adds. "But no one has ever created quite this amount of—"

"Damage," Kenny finishes her thought.

Mom asks, "But, a month for a complete accident?"

"You know what I always do in a situation like this?" Kenny asks, then pops a mini hot dog in his mouth, briskly rubs his hands together to get off any remaining flaky crust, chews, and swallows. "I look on the bright side."

"There's a bright side?" Mom asks.

"There's always a bright side, dear," Carmella says.

Kenny says, "It's nearly December. You're in the northern-most US Christmas mecca. You're going to work outside on a tree farm and get to soak up crisp, fresh air. And you haven't even met the local teens yet."

"Oh, such nice kids," Carmella says. "You'll like them."

"But they won't like me," I say. "Everyone here hates me."

Carmella tilted her head. "Give it a wee bit of time. They'll come around."

"What about school?" I ask.

"The chief justice took the liberty of calling your school and arranging a cyber program for you," Mom says. "And she offered to personally tutor you, if you need help with anything. If she hadn't found Brady guilty and sentenced her to live here for the month, I might think she was actually a nice woman. I only hope those ladies in your school's office don't start a whole gossip train at home, what with the bazaar coming up and everything." Then Mom gasps, "Oh no! The bazaar!" She explains to the Crispins, "I'm the chairwoman. It's an honor, really. But a huge responsibility too. Everyone is counting on me. It's a major fundraiser." She looks at my dad. "What will happen to it?"

"Well, maybe you can fly back and forth?" Carmella suggests. "There's a small airport just over the border in Canada that's much closer than Niagara Falls International."

"Oh, I don't know." Mom says, "I'm in charge of . . . well, I'm in charge of everything."

"I'll be fine, Mom. Go home," I say. "The bazaar needs you."

"We'll take very good care of her," Carmella says. "No need to worry. What am I saying? Of course, you'll worry; you're a mom. That's your job."

I look at my mom and dad. "It'll be OK."

❄ ❄ ❄

In my Yuletide bedroom, I pick up my phone, which is all charged up.

Brady Bancroft GUILTY!

Justice served!

"Geez." I scroll down a little, and I can't believe what I see. A video of the whole court thing, including my charges and sentencing. Someone recorded it and posted it? "That's so mean," I say to myself.

Should have been worse!

It won't bring back our tree.

And she's staying!?

Who the heck wants her to stay around and do more damage?!

CHAPTER 11

Mom shakes me awake in the middle of the night. She's fully dressed and has makeup on. "Brady, we can leave. Right now."

My mind is hazy, but I understand what she's proposing. "Like a fugitive?"

"No," Mom says. "We talked to our lawyer. He said none of this was official. We could just leave this frozen tundra of a town and forget about it."

I sit up and look around. She and Dad have my bags all packed.

"I can't go," I say.

"Sure, you can. We have four-wheel drive."

"I feel so terrible about what I did. I ruined the tree farm's Christmas business. Mr. Schneider expected to make enough money to repay the taxes, and then Dad wouldn't be able to buy the farm, and he could keep it. I ruined all of that. I think maybe doing what the chief justice says might make me feel better."

Mom asks, "You mean you want to stay here?"

"Yeah. I think it will be OK, like Carmella said."

CHAPTER 12

enny drops me off at Schneider's Tree Farm at 8:45 a.m. He says it will make a good impression to be a little early. And maybe he's right because Mr. Schneider actually looks a little glad to see me.

"Bancroft girl!" he calls to me. "Good thing you're here. We just had half the staff call out with the flu." He looks at my Chuck Taylors and wipes his hand over his face. "Those won't work."

"Sorry. I don't have boots."

"Jay!" he calls into a barn in need of a paint job.

A boy comes out. Not any boy, the cute boy from the sleigh. He's in a red Schneider's Tree Farm sweatshirt that looks like it had been washed a hundred times. He wears a tight cap and thick work gloves. "Mr. S?"

"Jay, this is Bancroft. See if you can find her some boots."

"You got it. Follow me, Bancroft."

I have no problem with following Jay. It gives me a chance to check out his faded jeans from behind.

We walk into a tack room complete with all kinds of horse accessories: saddles, stirrups, harnesses, and helmets. There's a shelf on which sits a row of cowboy boots, riding boots, real high rubber boots that look like you could use them to wade in a creek, and rain boots.

"See anything that will fit?"

I choose a pair of well-worn Hunter rain boots and take off my sneakers, revealing today's hot-pink Hello Kitty socks.

At the sight of them, Jay says, "Yowza. Those are bright."

"Yeah. I guess they are."

"And really thin."

"Yeah. I guess they are."

"The key to staying warm working outside all day is to keep your head and feet warm and dry." He disappears for a minute and comes back with a pair of wool socks. "Try these. Tuck your jeans into them."

I put them on over my Hello Kitty ones and do like he said. Then I slide the boots on. They come to just below my knee.

"That should be good. Need a hat?" he asked.

I pull the striped stocking hat out of my pocket. "I have this."

"That'll work, if that's the way you wanna go."

I don't want to wear the hat, but it's my only option. "You have something better?"

"You know what? It's fine. It's functional, and it has character. Go with it."

I put the hat on.

Jay smirks.

I don't want to have character.

"It totally works for you. If anyone gives you a hard time about it, you tell me, and I'll take care of it."

I smile at that because not only is Jay cute, he's nice, and maybe he'll be my friend, which is something I figure I may need over the next month. I'm not excited, however, that he expects someone might give me a hard time. I'm having a hard enough time without anything being added to it.

Just then a girl walks in, breathing heavily, like she's been running. "Hey, Jay. What are you doing? We need you." She looks at me. Well, she looks at my hat. "Great, *you're* here." She looks at my feet. "And why are you wearing my boots?"

"I'm sorry. I didn't know they were yours."

Jay offers, "Mari, chill. She had sneakers, so your dad told me to hook her up with some boots. It's all good."

There is an awkward pause, which she breaks. "I came to get you for the lower field. Customers need you. And Bancroft, you can sweep up loose needles from the workshop over to the east side . . ."

Jay leaves without saying goodbye—so much for having a friend—bumping into another girl, whose nose is buried in an iPad, on his way out. "Sorry, Pepper," he says.

Pepper calls to him without looking up from the screen, "Hey, funny stuff, North. Thanks for sharing."

"Yeah. Right," he says, and he disappears.

I don't know what she's talking about, of course . . . seems normal that they have inside jokes and stuff.

Pepper taps the screen. "Our margins are up, but volume is down, so we're holding steady. We need to—" She stops when she sees me. "Oh, *you're* here."

Mari says, "She's going to sweep."

I pause, but don't move.

Pepper says, "Sweeping seems harmless."

"Right. Umm, where's the workshop?"

Mari rolls her eyes. "Just follow the signs that say Workshop."

Pepper adds, "Cool hat." Her smirk tells me she things its anything but cool.

It's going to be a long month.

I see a broom, snatch it, and head toward the workshop. Pepper gives Mari more tree sales information, when Jay suddenly reappears. He tosses me a pair of thick leather gloves, caked with dirt.

"You'll need these."

CHAPTER 13

M y pile is big and there isn't a stray needle to be found. While I wait for the next needle to fall, I sit on a stump and check my phone.

I never should've checked because I can't believe what I see . . . more posts and photos about me . . . from today, working here!

Look at the girl who ruined Christmas

If you're wondering what the punishment looks like for destroying Christmas for Harper Hollow Falls . . .

If you're looking for a laugh, come out to Schneider's Tree Farm and watch the Girl Who Ruined Christmas sweep.

Sigh.

Doesn't anyone in this town have anything better to do than harass me?

"I guess you haven't worked before." Mari is suddenly behind me and I think I just said that out loud. "But here we don't play on our phones during business hours. Yeah, we're funny that way about working while we're at work. Weird, huh?"

I quickly shove the phone in my pocket. "Is there something else you want me to do?"

Mari adjusts the big box of bows she has propped against her hip and surveys my perfect needle pile. "For starters, you have to move that pile. It's a fire hazard this close to the shed. Unless . . ." She eyes me. "Maybe that was your plan . . . to start another fire."

I can't believe she thinks that. "Of course not."

Mari leaves with her bows, and I move the needles behind the shed. I concentrate on doing a good job. When I look up, there's a group of customers looking and clicking pictures of me with their phones.

That's when I get an idea . . . maybe I can help fix what I ruined. I set the broom aside and wave to Pepper in the group of onlookers. "Come here," I say.

She follows me to the side of the barn. "What is it?"

"Those people came here to see me."

"I know. They're fascinated."

"So, that's your money-maker."

"What is?" she asks.

"Me!"

Pepper looks at the customers who have come to see me, but they're doing something else while they're here. They're shopping. They buy wreaths, hot cocoa, lights, and ornaments. "They're spending money."

"Exactly," I say. "Let's lean into it."

"Yes. Great idea. The upsell." Pepper addresses the group, "Catch a glimpse of the Girl Who Ruined Christmas. Please be sure to tag Schneider's Tree Farm in your posts."

I go back to sweeping, occasionally looking up for a picture, when Jay drives up in a golf cart with snow tires decked out like a full Christmasmobile, with lights and garland. He's toting a family of three, and their tree is tied to the roof.

While he's handing the mother a tag, I hear him say, "Here, you can pay for this inside," but he's watching me out of the corner of his eye. He smiles to the woman. "I'll get this tied onto your car. Thanks for your business."

When the woman walks into the workshop, he says to Pepper, "You've got a month to make her miserable, you don't have to get it all done in one day."

Pepper answers, "Are you kidding me? That court-house video is going viral. People are interested in the Girl

Who Ruined Christmas. This was her idea, although I probably would've thought of it myself."

"I just sent someone in to pay. Can you manage the register, like you're supposed to?"

"Sure. But this is grassroots marketing at its finest." Pepper walks away, then turns to add, "Don't forget, Jay North, we're trying to keep this place open."

CHAPTER 14

I sit in the corner of the workshop at the end of the day, waiting for someone to ask me to do something or to tell me it's OK to call Kenny to pick me up. My teeth have finally stopped chattering. I take a minute to return Mom's and Dad's texts and let them know that everything is fine.

Mari reorganizes the wreaths for sale on the walls.

Pepper is at the register, counting money and making notes on her iPad.

Jay walks in, holding a clipboard and making check marks.

Finally, Mr. Schneider comes in and slides off his gloves. He asks Pepper, "How are we compared to this day last year?"

Mari says, "Up by fifteen trees."

Pepper taps her screen, "Once all the numbers are in, it could be more like seventeen. Three of them were the ten-foot Frasers, and the margin on those is fifty percent."

Jay says, "Certainly feels like it's been hopping all day. There's a buzz of excitement in the air."

"Jay, cover your ears if you don't want to hear this," Mari says. Then to her dad and Pepper, she says, "I'm telling you, people are totally curious about her."

Does she know I'm sitting right here, and I can hear this?

"We might even get some Canadians to make the trek to check her out." Pepper flips a thumb in my direction, so, yeah, I guess she does know I'm here, but she doesn't care that I can hear her.

Mr. Schneider turns his faded baseball hat around backwards and rubs his hands on his ginger beard. "Pepper, look—"

But Pepper interrupts him. "I have some ideas on boosting sales inside the store—"

He walks into the backroom, but Pepper follows him. ". . . we'll optimize the increased foot traffic . . ."

There's a beat of awkwardness when it's just me, Mari and Jay. Mari says, "I'm going to go turn out the lights." Then to me she says, "You can wear the boots home, if you want, but bring them back tomorrow."

She leaves before hearing me thank her.

Now it's only me and Jay.

"I guess that means I'm free to go."

"Yeah. We're done for today."

I take my phone out and begin dialing Kenny Crispin, but before I hit the call button, Jay adds, "If you're going to last the month, you're going to have to ignore them."

"I get that they're mad," I say. "I'd be mad at me too."

"I'm sure it's hard, but try to chill," he says.

"I can totally do that. You know, Southern Cal kind of invented chill." After the words come out, I think that maybe I shouldn't try to be cute.

Jay raises a brow, "Is that so?"

Or maybe cute is OK. "Totally," I say. "It's in every movie and song that references chill. I mean, when was the last time a song was written about Harper Hollow?"

"Falls."

"Falls?"

"It's Harper Hollow Falls. It references the waterfalls that flow from the river. And I'm pretty sure California didn't *invent* chill. We chill just fine here."

"You do?"

"Sure. I guess you don't know that song?" He sings, slaps his knee and stomps his foot. "Hey, Harper Hollow. Hey, Harper Hollow Falls! You're so chill, Harper Hollow . . . Falls."

It's terrible. I mean, a really bad tune sung in a terrible voice.

I chuckle. "You'd never survive in my a cappella group."

"That's OK. I don't think that's a group I want to be in."

Then seriously I say, "Thanks, Jay."

"For what?"

"You're the only one here that's nice to me. I mean, except for the Crispins, of course."

He smiles. "Say, I'm heading out to do some ice fishing after I'm done here if you want to, you know, chill."

Ice fishing? It sounds cold and fishy and . . . "Great," I say. "I love fishing. And I love ice, so . . . sounds perfect."

CHAPTER 15

Well, if there is one place I never thought I'd be, it's on a frozen lake, in a hut with a hole cut into its floor. To my surprise, though, "hut" undersells this place. It's more like a tiny cabin. The walls and built-in benches are wood, and there's a wood-burning stove that keeps the place warm, almost cozy. Jay put a red plaid blanket under my butt and another on my lap. I expected to be freezing, but I'm not.

Then it's on to fishing. I've never been before. Thankfully, Jay baited my hook for me. Then he dropped it in the hole. Now I'm just holding on to it and waiting. Really, it's a very easy sport, borderline boring.

Jay says, "Tell me about Cali."

"Let's see. I have a best friend named Lou Lou. We're in the same singing group at school. And we hang out pretty much every day."

"You miss her?"

"I do. She's awesome. I can't imagine her ever treating anyone like Mari and Pepper did today."

"You aren't going to believe me, but they aren't usually like that. They're protective of the farm. I think it'll wear off in a few days."

"I can't believe they recorded the court hearing and then posted it."

"Oh, right, that," Jay says. "I think that spiraled out of control. How could anyone know it would go viral?"

"Whatever," I say. "I'm taking your advice, and I'm chilling. Besides, if my viral video helps bring business to the farm, then I guess it's worth it."

"But if the farm makes enough money to pay off the back taxes, it'll mess up your dad's real estate deal, and there will be one less sneaker factory in the world," Jay says.

"There's always another location for a factory," I say. "Do you think that could happen—that they'll sell enough trees to make the money they need?"

"I hope they do. But I don't think it's possible. Even if every single person in Harper Hollow Falls bought a tree, it wouldn't be enough. That's why they want to get people to come from Porter City, but it's hard for them to get here. Maybe with the video and the excitement over you, people will make the trek, like Pepper said."

"She seems to have a good mind for business." Then I ask, "Why is it so hard for the people from Porter City to get here? It's not that far."

"It's not far at all; it's only across the river, but there's no bridge nearby, so it's a pain to drive to the nearest one."

There are a few awkward beats of silence when neither of us talks. In the quiet, we hear carolers in the distance. "This is one of my favorites," I say when I hear, "'Chestnuts roasting on an open fire . . .'"

We listen for a second, and then a knock at the door, it makes us jump.

The door opens, and standing there, bundled up from head to toe in green and red layers, is Carmella Crispin. She brought cookies. Steam floats off the top of the plate; they're fresh from the oven.

"Hi, kids," she says. "I thought you might be hungry."

Jay says, "You know me, Mrs. Crispin, I'm always hungry."

She giggles, thrilled with the idea. "Don't I know it."

The something else happens. My fishing pole bends.

"You got a bite!" Jay calls.

CHAPTER 16

The next day at the farm I sweep needles behind the
shed without being told.

As Jay predicted, Pepper and Mari pay less attention
to me today. Occasionally they walk past, each time Pepper
is rattling off a different get-rich-quick idea:

"You only need one kidney, so we could sell the
other . . ."

"The lottery . . ."

"I'm just saying, *if* we were to rob a bank . . ."

Tree buyers arrive, and many flash pictures of me.
One lady says, "Excuse me, but are you the girl . . . you
know, the one who . . ."

"Am I the Girl Who Ruined Christmas? Yeah, that
would be me," I say, trying to be a good sport.

She smiles. "Oh wow. Could I get a shot of you with my kids?"

Good sport . . . good sport. "Sure," I say.

Pepper spots me posing. After the mom thanks me, Pepper grabs my arm. "Genius idea," she says. She leads me to a space in front of the workshop that nicely displays the wreaths for sale. "Wait here," she says.

I do.

She returns a minute later with a sign:

THE GIRL WHO RUINED CHRISTMAS
SCHNEIDER'S TREE FARM
HARPER HOLLOW FALLS, NY

She hands me the sign and calls in to the customers milling about shopping or in line to pay, saying, "Step right up. Step right up. Get your free photo with the Girl Who Ruined Christmas." People perk up at the idea, almost as if admitting that this is why they're here in the first place.

Pepper continues, "The line forms here."

I hold the sign, and people stand to my right and left to get the shot. Some of them ask me questions:

"Do you hate Christmas?"

"Do you hate Clydesdales?"

"Do you hate the cider at Blitzen's?"

Not sure how to answer these things, I go along with my new role. I drop a few "Bah, humbugs," and a "Yuck, cider." Those seem to get laughs.

They love it!

Pepper tells them, "Hashtag that 'Schneider's Christmas Tree Farm' and save two dollars on a wreath." She hands out coupons when people show her their posts.

There's a buzz around the workshop; everyone seems excited and laughing, and most importantly, they're spending money. Mari is behind me, ringing up wreath after wreath. People ask her if they have Girl Who Ruined Christmas T-shirts.

❄ ❄ ❄

The hubbub makes the day go fast.

While I sit on a split-rail fence waiting for Carmella to pick me up, I quickly call home since my mom's been blowing up my phone with worry. I assure her everything is OK. Luckily, she doesn't see any of the social media from here.

Then I hear Pepper inside the workshop brainstorming the ways she can exploit my popularity for the benefit of the business.

She says, "If it snows tonight, we can charge people to throw snowballs at her tomorrow."

Jay says, "We're not going to do that."

I guess I'm excited that I can help in some small way, but that doesn't sound fun.

Carmella arrives in the truck. She takes one look at me and says, "I know what you need."

And I know what she knows I need.

CHAPTER 17

*C*armella and I are elbow-deep in gingerbread dough. I'm rolling and pressing and molding and cutting. "Did you call your Mom today?" she asks. "I'm sure she misses you."

"I did, and yes, she does."

Carmella has every kind of edible decoration you can imagine. I'm totally lost in my thoughts and focused on my cookie project when Kenny comes home.

He looks at my work and whistles. "Oh my word!"

I step back and look at the gingerbread house I've built. It's a miniature model of the workshop at the tree farm. I've even written "Schneider's" in icing on a little sign.

I tilt my head to get a good look at it. "It did come out good, huh?"

"Amazing," Kenny says. "It's a replica. You have a real talent."

"Better than good," Carmella says as she walks over from the oven with a cookie sheet on which she has six tiny gingerbread wreaths.

"Oh, that's perfect!" I say. And I add them to the workshop. "I'm going to give this to the girls tomorrow. Do you think they'll like it?"

"They'll love it!" Kenny says. "But it may still take them a little while to warm up to you."

"Don't you worry," Carmella says, "They'll come around."

"Maybe this gingerbread creation will help," Kenny says.

❄ ❄ ❄

I'm excited and nervous to bring the miniature cookie replica to the farm the next day. Maybe Pepper and Mari will see it as a peace offering and want to be friends. Or maybe they'll find something to hate about it and launch straight into today's profitable ways to humiliate me.

No one's around when I set the gingerbread workshop down, so I fetch the broom and get to work. On my way, I pass the recycling bin, which is filled with papers, mostly newspapers and advertisements. There's a flyer right on top that catches my eye. I reach in and, wouldn't you know it, *that's* when Pepper arrives.

"You a garbage picker too, Brady?" she asks.

I ignore her and read the flyer. It's for the Northeast Ice Sculpture Contest.

"Did you see this?" I hold it out for Pepper. With all of her schemes, how could she miss this one? "The prize is twenty-five thousand dollars."

"Of course. I thought about it, but that takes *skills* . . . skills we don't have. They get entries from all over, from people who are really good."

I'm not as ready to dismiss this as she is. I think:

Sandcastles . . .
Gingerbread houses . . .
Ice sculptures!
How different can they be?

Mari enters with new wreathes hooked up each of her arms from wrist to shoulder. "We need to get these hung up in here."

Pepper and I each take some and start hanging them on the empty wall hooks. Once Mari's hands are empty, she wipes them on her jeans and turns to see my cookie model of the workshop.

"Where did this come from?" she asks.

Pepper says, "I don't know. It was here when I got here. It's cute, isn't it?"

Mari says, "Like really cute."

"Wonder how it tastes," Pepper says just as Jay enters.

"Taste? You need something tasted?" he asks.

"A gingerbread house," Mari says.

"It's your lucky day. I'm kind of an expert at cookies." He takes one of the little wreaths from the model, and before he pops it in his mouth, he says, "It's almost too pretty to eat." And he throws it in. "*Almost . . .*"

We wait for his reaction.

It only takes a second for the receptors in his tongue to send a message to his brain that says, *delicious!*

He "Mmmms" and takes another wreath, but Mari knocks it out of his hand.

"Don't eat them. People will love this," she says. "Where did it come from?"

"I . . ." I hesitate. "I made it last night. Kind of a peace offering, since saying 'I'm sorry' seems to fall on deaf ears."

Pepper asks, "What's that? I can't hear you."

I sigh.

I guess it isn't going to help.

Jay says, "Well, I love it."

Mari and Pepper lean over the iPad to look at today's work schedule, when I say, "You know, there's this contest.

The Northeast Ice Sculpture Contest. And, well, I know you said you don't have the skills, but I'm pretty good at designing those kinds of things. I've never done it with ice before, but I also had never done it with gingerbread before last night. Only sand."

The three look at each other. They don't agree to it, but they don't shoot down the idea completely, either.

So I add, "If we all work together, maybe we can help the farm."

Jay speaks first. "It's not a terrible idea."

Mari says, "It's worth a try."

Pepper exhales loudly. "Fine. We'll enter, but this is a long shot."

CHAPTER 18

I call Kenny and Carmella during the day to get them up to speed and ask if I can invite the kids over to the Yuletide tonight to practice.

Kenny says: "I'll have everything all ready for you guys."

Carmella says: "And I'll have a hot dinner waiting for you."

Mr. Schneider says we can leave early, and also lets Jay borrow the golf cart to drive us to the Crispins'.

Carmella is waiting at the bay window and claps when we arrive.

The front door flies open. Kenny, today in a neon-yellow track jacket, waves us in. "Hurry, there's so much to do." He sees Mari struggling with a big metal toolbox, and he helps her.

Mari says, "My dad put that together for us. He says it should be everything we need."

"I'll put it out back," Kenny says.

We each take a bowl of Carmella's signature tater tot casserole and a fistful of cookies and follow Kenny to the backyard. The pergola is well lit with hundreds of white lights, and Kenny already has a big block of ice on the picnic table.

Mari uses both arms to hoist the toolbox onto the table. She opens it, studies its contents, and tells us, "OK. We got chisels, files, drills, hammers . . ." She holds something up that looks like a cheese grater. "And this thing. I don't know what it is, but it could come in handy."

I take a Sharpie out of the box and draw on the tablecloth.

The girls and Jay watch as they eat cheese, tater tots, and cookies. I explain my vision for the sculpture, and why I think we should go with this design. "We know this better than anyone."

No one disagrees.

"Let's get started," I say.

We chop and cut and shave.

Carmella comes out periodically to refill our plates.

When I hear her call from the kitchen, "A little help?" I go in to see what's up. She's made hot chocolate with little marshmallows.

"You think of everything." I take two of the mugs, but I don't move. "Carmella, thank you for everything."

"They're just marshmallows." She giggles.

"I meant *everything*."

She smiles, and I note how rosy the balls of her cheeks are. "Oh dear, I enjoy this so much." Then she asks, "Are you having fun with your new friends?"

"I am," I say, and realize it's the first moment of fun I've had since I arrived. But "friends"? I guess to anyone not familiar with the situation who looked at us out there, sculpting and eating and occasionally laughing, they could think maybe we were friends. But I know better.

The sculpture slowly takes shape. It's a Christmas tree—well, almost.

Pepper asks, "How do we get the star to not look . . . lopsided?"

I say, "We need a more precise tool than a chisel."

Mari digs into her tool chest and comes up with a small power tool. "This puppy has attachments for sanding and sawing. All different sizes." She lowers safety goggles onto her face, stands on the table, and works at the top of the tree with the tool.

I walk around the table to get a good view of the star from every side, "Just a little more off the left point."

Mari revs up the tool and goes at it.

The ice cracks and the side of the star falls off.

"Oh no!" Pepper says.

Mari jumps off the table, lifts the goggles, and looks at what she's done. "Drat!"

I say, "That's why we're practicing."

Then the entire sculpture cracks down the middle and falls in half. Big chunks of ice hit the weathered picnic table and its wood splinters.

Mari says, "We're doomed."

"Great idea, Calamity Cali," Pepper says. "What do you know about ice anyway? You never even saw ice until a week ago."

I decide to push back this time. "At least I'm trying for realistic ways to get the money."

Jay says, "Brady has a point."

Pepper says, "Organ donation is big business."

Kenny appears, and he's dragging another block of ice behind him like an ox would pull a plow. "I planned for just such an emergency," he says. "With a back-up."

Jay helps him slide it over to the table wreckage.

Kenny says, "Try again."

I rip off a piece of the tablecloth and make a new design.

Everyone agrees to give it a try.

Mari revs up her power tool—she clearly loves power tools—and slides the goggles back on.

Snowflakes spew out from all around the sculpture. Jay films it on his phone.

I put some finishing touches on the sculpture and finally back away to reveal a symmetrical Christmas tree complete with a star, ornaments, and packages.

Mari and Pepper nod, and I can't believe it happens, but they offer me a fist bump.

Jay smiles at the sight of it, then pulls me into a hug. A hug!

Mari looks at our amazing work. "*That* deserves a celebration."

"For sure," Pepper agrees. "Tomorrow morning, Blitzen's Café."

We agree to meet before the tree farm opens at noon.

CHAPTER 19

I'm a little nervous to go to Blitzen's Café; after all, they think I maliciously destroyed their huge front window. But I'm excited to meet the group . . . "the group." Am I part of a local friend group?

The café is the cutest thing ever. It's reindeer everything, everywhere: reindeer wall art, antler chandeliers and table legs, menus shaped like reindeer heads, and every wooden chair is engraved with a reindeer's name.

The front window has already been replaced and has new decals—the lyrics to "Rudolph, the Red-Nosed Reindeer"—stuck to it.

Mari, Pepper, and Jay are sitting in a booth next to the fireplace, complete with stockings hung.

When I sit (in a chair engraved with "Vixen"), Jay slides a mug of yellowish-brownish steaming liquid over to me. I smell it, not sure what it is.

Pepper offers, "It's only the best hot cider ever." I think that's the first time she's spoken to me first. And it wasn't anything snarky.

Should I worry that she's put something in it?

Like something that in twenty minutes will have me running to the bathroom?

Nah, Jay wouldn't let that happen.

I've never been a huge cider fan. I mean, it's thick apple juice, and apple juice reminds me of kindergarteners with snot dripping from their noses.

I sip.

All three look at me for my reaction.

Oh. Em. I mean . . . OH! EM!

My eyes feel like they're popping out of my head.

"Yeah," I say. "The. Best. Cider. Ever."

They smile, satisfied by my opinion.

I take another sip then ask, "So what do you all do in the summer?"

Jay asks, "What's that?"

It takes me a second to catch on that he's joking and laugh.

Mari says, "Our summers are only about a month long."

"Actually, summer is the same length of time everywhere, it's just that our temperatures are only summer-like for about three to four weeks," Pepper explains.

Jay adds, "Once the snow melts, we spend about two months slopping around in mud and muck, and then the trees and flowers explode with so much color it hurts your eyes."

There's excitement in their voices, making it so obvious how much they love Harper Hollow Falls.

Mari says, "We play baseball, ride bikes, camp out . . . the usual."

I sip and say, "I've never been camping."

All three of them in unison ask, "Seriously!?"

Jay says, "You'll have to come back and give it a try."

Did I just hear an invitation to return? I thought they couldn't wait to get rid of me.

I say, "If my dad's deal goes through—" Oh crap. I wince and wish I could reel that back. "I mean if he works out a way to make a deal and keep the tree farm open . . ."

The fun vibe is gone. The whole mood shifts.

After a beat of quiet, Jay says, "Hey, we still have a little time before we have to be to work. And I have to buy my mom a gift for Christmas—"

Christmas?

Shopping?

I've been so preoccupied I haven't done any shopping. Of all the places in the world to let Christmas shopping slip my mind . . .

Jay says, "Let's go."

We walk a few doors down to Garland, Greetings and Gifts. It's like a general store that has a little bit of everything. I easily fill my basket with gifts for everyone.

I notice that Mari and Pepper look, but don't select anything.

Pepper flips through a leather planner. She says, "This is a great design. I've been looking for a way to keep all of my ideas organized." She turns it over, glances at the price, then puts it back.

Mari tries on a pair of gloves. "These are like wearing clouds. My hands get so rough from working outside all the time. I look at my dad's hands and worry those will be mine someday."

I say, "They're cute."

Mari takes them off and puts them back.

Then Pepper looks into my basket. "You've got a small fortune there."

"Just a few presents for my family and the Crispins. My dad left me some spending money."

I take a cute little figurine of a singing elf off a shelf. "My friend Lou Lou will love this. We have the same taste . . ."

Jay walks up behind me without me hearing him, and startles me when he asks, "Who is the keychain for?"

I look at the keychain in my basket. "Oh, my mom. She's always losing her keys."

"That's cool, same with me. I've been wondering if those key finder gadgets actually work."

Now I'm all self-conscious, because I know I stand out with my full basket, while everyone else is empty handed, but I thought we were going shopping. It would be weird if I put the stuff back.

I say, "I'll just go pay."

As I walk away, I hear Pepper say to Mari, "Must be nice."

Mari says, "She's from a different world, face it."

Jay jumps in. "Guys, she's making an effort."

Equally upset and encouraged by what I hear, I put the gifts on the counter and pay as quickly as possible.

On my way out of the store I pause at a sign with the store's hours:

OPEN TILL 8:00 P.M.

THROUGH CHRISTMAS EVE.

CHAPTER 20

T hat night I'm in my room at the Yuletide, the one with the red gingham plaid curtains, wrapping some gifts. I'm making a tag that reads, "To: Jay," when Carmella knocks on my door.

"Come in."

She's in a full-length nightgown and matching cap. "Hello, sweetheart. I just wanted to check on you. You've been quiet tonight. How are you doing?"

"I'm OK."

"Just OK? You know the big day is coming soon."

"I can't seem to get in the Christmas spirit, which is weird because it's literally everywhere." I bring Jay's gift over to the others that I've labeled for Mari, Pepper, and the Crispins. On the floor, near my suitcase, I have other gifts wrapped for Mom and Dad and Lou Lou.

Carmella says, "It sure looks like you're trying, but I didn't mean Christmas; we all know that's coming, whether we're ready or not. I meant the ice sculpture contest."

"Oh, yeah. That. I really hope that can help me clear my name."

Carmella says, "It seems that the others have warmed up to you nicely."

I pick up my phone and tap it to show Carmella clips of me at the Christmas tree farm on social media and the comments people have been writing.

She sits next to me on the bed and looks over my shoulder. Then I click to the one from the trial. "This is the one that started it all."

"I don't really understand all that social mumbo jumbo, but I can give you a hug. Would that help?"

"A hug would be great," I say.

"Don't let despair get in the way. I'm sure the friends you've made see the real you."

I say, "It certainly wouldn't hurt to win that prize money and fix what I broke."

"You know, all of this business with the farm and the taxes . . . it's a big thing that was all in motion before you arrived, so you can't put this on yourself, Brady. It's bigger than you." She moves toward the door. "And I wish you lots of luck in the contest tomorrow, but it might take more than winning a contest to fix such a complicated situation."

CHAPTER 21

*T*he big day arrives. Not Christmas Day, the other big day.

Every one of the 1,100 people from Harper Hollow Falls is at the park with sturdy Stan McSpruce watching over the Northeast Ice Sculpture Contest.

Picnic tables are roped off, inaccessible to anyone except the contestants. The tables are covered in white paper, and each has a giant block of ice in the middle.

Our team of four wears matching Schneider's Christmas Tree Farm shirts. Pepper said it was an advertising opportunity, and we shouldn't miss it. Dan Schneider and the Crispins are nearby for support and cookies as needed.

The other tables are manned by out-of-towners.

Two of the groups have branded fleece jackets with their team names: the Shavers from Buffalo, New York, and the Cubes from Canada. The fourth team looks like they just came from Alaska, dressed in matching fur-lined caps and boots.

Carmella dawdles by the tables, checking out the competition, as Mayor Winter blows a whistle. Not satisfied with everyone's attentiveness to her whistle, she raises her megaphone and blows her whistle into it.

That does it.

Mayor Winter says, "Places, everyone!"

Then she shoos Carmella away from our table so that she doesn't disturb the carving teams.

Using her megaphone, she says, "All righty-roos. I'm your commentator. Here are the rules: Each team will be judged on creativity, complexity, and overall amount of ice surface. That means that if you whittle your block down to an icicle, you won't win any points. You have one hour. On your marks, get set, go!"

She blows her whistle into the megaphone and ducks away from the flurries that instantly shoot out from everyone tooling at their blocks.

I display the drawing of the tree design we've agreed on. Jay, Mari, and Pepper don their goggles and begin to chisel.

Meanwhile, the Cubes from Canada let their leader start working with a giant blade. He cracks their block into smaller cubes that each team member works on with their own tools.

The Shavers each take a side of their cube, and with planers, they shave curls of ice, letting them refreeze.

The Furry Foreigners use super pointy ice picks and meticulously poke at their block.

The entire roped-off area is a blizzard of ice shavings.

"One minute left," Mayor Winter calls through her megaphone.

That was seriously the Fastest. Hour. Of. My. Life.

I glance at the opposing teams, who shield their creations from view.

Pepper and Mari do the same with ours. And we all throw silver tarps over our sculptures as Mayor Winter blows her whistle. "Time!" she shouts. "Put your tools down and step away from your table."

A team of three judges with clipboards examines the work.

Mayor Winter, Mr. Schneider, and the Crispins wiggle into the restricted area to be right near our table.

The judges move to the Furry Foreigners' table, where we see they have sculpted an igloo with an Eskimo family and seals.

It's very detailed and cute. Oohs and aahs come from the crowd.

Mari whispers, "Seals? Seriously?"

After some discussion and notes, the judges move to our team. We've added a lot more detail since rehearsal,

including a tag that reads "Schneider's Tree Farm," which took Mari like twenty minutes, and candy canes on the tree. Lastly, at Kenny's suggestion, we've propped a multi-colored laser light nearby and projected it onto the sculpture. It's a really good touch.

The notes and discussion among the judges are quick.

Pepper asks us, "Do you think it's good or bad if they're fast? Like, maybe a no-brainer that we won? Or a no-brainer that we lost?"

I shrug.

Jay takes off his hat; he's sweating.

I look at Mari's hands; she's bitten her nails all the way down.

The tarp is removed from the Shavers' ice sculpture.

It's a beautiful angel with wings that look like actual feathers, made from curled shavings.

The crowd gasps and claps.

"How did they do that?" Pepper asks.

Dan tosses his red Schneider's hat on the ground, and Carmella shoves a cookie in his mouth.

The judges scribble notes and move to the Cubes.

The tarp is removed to reveal an elaborate snowflake made entirely out of individually shaped ice cubes that are stuck together with ice. The edges give it a dimensional glistening that actually picks up Kenny's lights.

Kenny's mouth hangs open. "That's amazing."

Carmella kicks Kenny.

Pepper takes off her goggles and sets them on the table. She looks at me and shakes her head. "I knew we didn't have the skills for this. I told you."

Mari adds, "And now you've done it again."

Jay says, "Guys, it's not her fault."

"Yeah, it is," Pepper says. "All of this is."

Pepper and Mari leave.

I pick up the laser light, and Jay cleans up the tools.

The Cubes get their medals and hoot and holler at their win.

Jay says, "Sorry."

I can't help but blink back tears. I'm glad Mari and Pepper aren't here to see this, and I really don't want Jay to see me cry.

I turn and see Carmella Crispin. She opens her arms, and I can't hold it in any longer. I fall into them and sob.

CHAPTER 22

The farm feels different the next morning. It's dark, quiet, and gloomy.

Someone, I'm guessing Pepper by the handwriting, made a sign:

December 22nd

Going Out of Business

After 42 Years

I made three new gingerbread houses last night—Carmella's way of cheering me up. And it worked at the time, but now—not so much. In fact, holding them on this big board is awkward, like I'm showing up at a cake party with spaghetti.

Jay unwinds a garland on the golf cart.

I say to him, "I can help once I take this inside."

He says, "Thanks, but I got it."

"Oh." Seems like he's mad at me too. I go inside, knowing I've been snubbed.

Then he calls to me, "Brady—" I turn to hear him out. "Look, I'm sorry. I know it's not your fault, we were just . . . hopeful, that's all."

I say, "I get it. You'll all be rid of me tomorrow."

"Jeez. That only makes me feel worse."

I force half my lips to curl into a smile and move toward the workshop, but then turn back to tell him, "Oh, Mrs. Crispin wanted me to remind you that her annual Christmas social is on for tonight."

"*Social*?" he asks, confused by the word.

"Yeah. She's afraid if she calls it a 'party,' no one will come because they won't be in a mood to celebrate. She was going to cancel, but she thought everyone could use the cookies."

Jay nods, and flatly offers, "I guess I can always use cookies."

"Let me know if there's anything I can do."

Mari walks around the corner with a big box of glittery pinecones. "Haven't you done enough?"

Sigh.

Just one more day.

I set the gingerbread houses on the display counter and make a price tag for each. *Every little bit will help, right?*

Mari and Pepper busy themselves, but don't talk to me or each other.

The twinkle lights aren't blinking, so I switch them on.

❄ ❄ ❄

Mr. Schneider comes out of the office and turns on the Christmas music. "As hard as it will be, cheer up, everyone. It's our last day. Let's make it a good one. I want to thank everyone for your help. It's been a real team effort."

Then he looks at the gingerbread houses. "Where did these come from?"

"I made them last night. With Mrs. Crispin."

Mr. Schneider breaks a tiny piece off and eats it. "Delicious. And they look great." He leans closer to one of the houses that has gingerbread people. One of them is wearing a red cap. "Is that supposed to be me?

Everyone takes a closer look, and they all get a laugh at the resemblance.

"I'll bring that one home," he says.

I light up a little inside at the compliments.

❄ ❄ ❄

That evening, everyone from town mingles at the Yuletide B&B's annual Christmas social. Some people even manage to smile as they nibble on Carmella's food.

By the fireplace, a trio of carolers sing a downbeat version of "Silent Night."

Carmella hustles around the house, playing hostess. At one point, someone spills a little Poinsettia Punch. She's at the ready to save a cell phone that's within range of the spill and cleans it in a jiff.

No one talks to me, so I casually fade into the background and make my way upstairs to pack. I carefully bury the gifts for my parents and Lou Lou in my suitcase. And consider what to do with the things I bought for Mari, Pepper, and Jay. It feels weird to go downstairs and give them to them now, so I set them on the dresser. I take the gifts for the Crispins downstairs and try to be invisible as I maneuver through the crowd.

After successfully tucking the gifts underneath the tree, I plan to find Carmella to see if I can help with anything, but as I turn away from the tree, I see that Mr. Schneider is staring at it. Kenny comes up behind him.

"Sure is a beaut," Kenny says, and hands Mr. Schneider a glass of eggnog.

"At least I can say we produced a banner crop our last year . . . there wasn't a bad tree on the whole lot, no matter what kind."

I don't want to be in the conversation, but somehow I'm standing there with them. So I ask a question I've wondered about for a month. "Can I ask you something, Mr. Schneider?"

He sips his eggnog. "Sure."

"Why didn't you replace the White House tree with another one? Like you said, there were so many good ones to choose from."

Mr. Schneider bristles a bit at this, although I don't know why. It seems like a fair question.

Kenny steps in before Mr. Schneider can answer. "Brady, what's done is done."

"It's OK, she's not the first to wonder," Mr. Schneider breaks in. He continues, "The thing is, the White House sent a team to select *the* tree, and I thought about just putting a new one on a trailer and faking it after you started the fire—"

"Technically, I didn't—"

Mr. Schneider cuts me off. "When they called to confirm delivery, I told them not to worry, that we had the tree ready. But then they called back when they saw the courthouse video and told me that the White House didn't want to do business with someone who was less than honest." He pauses to sip his eggnog, then adds, "I'm so ashamed. First the taxes, then the tree lie, and now the farm closing."

I open my mouth to say something else, and Kenny's eyes tell me to drop it. I don't listen to Kenny's eyes. "Mr. Schneider, take it from someone who knows what it's like to have the whole world hate her, you have nothing to be ashamed of. Your family has been a part of the magic of Christmas for thousands of people for forty-two years . . . that's a lot to be proud of."

Kenny kisses me on the top of the head. "We're gonna miss you."

I thought maybe Mr. Schneider would agree about missing me, but he doesn't.

CHAPTER 23

December 23

My suitcase is packed, and I'm dressed in comfy traveling clothes. I grab a muffin for the road and pick up my cell phone, which is among the remaining items left to clean up from last night's social.

Carmella hurries in. "OK. Kenny has the car warmed up."

"Can I get a picture of us?"

"Oh, how sweet. Yes. Let's do one of those selfties." She pats her hair to make sure it's all in place.

I tap on the camera app, but it opens to pictures instead. *Hmm, I don't know these pictures.*

Many of them are of me, working at the farm. I scroll. And I find a video.

Not just any video.

The video. From the courtroom.

"How did this get on here?" I ask, more to myself than to Carmella.

"What is it, dear?"

I fiddle with the phone a little more and realize that this isn't my phone.

I ask her, "Where did this come from?" I show her the phone that looks like mine. "Whose is it?"

"Oh, that's Jay's. I rescued it from a Poinsettia Punch spill," she says.

"It was Jay," I tell her, my eyes welling up with tears. "Jay took that video of my sentencing and posted it so it could go viral. He fueled the fire that kept everyone hating me."

Carmella doesn't seem to know what to say. I expect she doesn't truly understand "post" or "viral."

Instead, she says, "You'll miss your flight, dear."

"Yeah. Right." Then I say to her, "You've done so much for me, and I can't thank you enough, but can I ask you to do one more favor for me?"

"Anything, dear."

"Will you give this back to Jay?"

"Of course," she says.

"And you can tell him that I saw everything."

CHAPTER 24

*W*ith the time difference, I get home with plenty of time to hang out with Lou Lou.

It feels good to be back in one of my favorite places—the mall!—with my best friend. I notice how differently California does Christmas. *I mean, pink trees?* And all the fake snow; these people have no idea how much it doesn't look like the real thing.

My phone rings: *JAY.*

I dismiss it.

Lou Lou says, "I still can't believe you served time."

I say, "I was truly only in lockup for like an hour, but still . . . yeah. It's a good story to tell my grandkids."

"Think your parents will sue?"

"My dad just wants to close the deal."

We weave through the crowd of last-minute shoppers and pick a food court table with a great view of outside—palm trees, packed parking lot, people with piles of boxes and bags.

Lou Lou's eyes are on her phone, and she asks, "Did All Hollows even have a mall?"

"Harper Hollow Falls," I correct her, while I scan the weather app to see what's happening in upstate New York: no surprise, flurries.

I say, "Actually, it wasn't so bad . . . they had these really cute stores all around the town square."

"Sounds old-fashioned."

I say, "I'd call it 'quaint,'" without lifting my eyes from the screen.

I shift from the weather app to stalk Pepper on social.

Lou Lou says, "Sounds like a nice way of saying old-fashioned."

Pepper's status says:

What should I have told the woman who insisted I give out a friend's phone number for a gingerbread house?

"Friend"?

I scroll through her posts, and ask Lou Lou, "What is?"

"What's what? Old fashioned? Are you even listening?"

I put the phone down. "Yeah, sorry, I just . . . no, it wasn't old fashioned. It was . . . cute."

"'Quaint' *and* 'cute'?"

"Yeah, I got your present at one of those cute, quaint little shops."

Lou Lou's eyes pop. "Present?"

"Of course."

She says, "Uh . . . what do you want for Christmas?"

I laugh a little. I guess if I'm out of sight, I'm out of mind. "Come on, I'll show you what I want." I drag her along until we're outside a store that neither of us has ever been in.

Bass Pro Shops.

Bass Pro Shops is a store with everything for hunting, fishing, and camping.

A second later, I'm demo-ing an ice fishing pole for Lou Lou.

I say, "You asked me what I wanted for Christmas."

"A fishing pole? Are you sure they didn't knock you around in prison?"

"It was kind of nice being outdoors every day," I say.

"We go outside every day."

"I mean all day. From sunup to sundown."

"Wasn't it cold?" she asks.

"Super cold. Kind of awesome, actually."

She shakes her head, confused. "I thought you said it was humiliating."

"Yeah. It was. But there were some fun moments, too."

I drag Lou Lou through the store and soon we're giggling, trying on high rubber boots and big hats with fishing lures hanging from them. I hand Lou Lou the pole so she can give it a feel for size and weight, just as Allie walks up with her dad.

She gets a laugh at the sight of us and clicks a pic on her phone.

"That's classic," she says.

It's like it's going to start all over again.

"Are you going to post that?" I snap at her.

"Jeez, Brady. Chill," she says. "No. I was just going to text it to you guys, so you'll have it." She holds her phone out to show me the pic of me and Lou Lou. "It's classic, don't you think?"

"Oh. Yeah. Sorry," I say.

Our phones vibrate.

"There. You have it," Allie says. "See you later."

She walks away and I say, "That was close."

"Very."

I point to a pole. "This one will be great."

"You seriously think I'm buying you a fishing pole for Christmas?" Lou Lou asks. "That's the kind of thing you write a letter to Santa to ask for."

A letter?

A switch flips in my brain.

I put the pole away and pull Lou Lou out of the store.

"You're a genius, Lou." I kiss her. "Man, I've missed you. A letter! Of course!"

Lou Lou says, "You do know there's no post office at the North Pole, right? I'm not even convinced there is a North Pole."

I say, "Oh, not to the North Pole. To the White House!"

She asks, "To the whole house, or is there a specific person?"

CHAPTER 25

I set up my laptop on my desk and prop Lou Lou in the chair.

She laces her fingers and cracks her knuckles. "OK. Lay it on me."

I dictate to her:

"Dear Mr. Flannigan—"

"Who's Flannigan?" Lou asks.

"He's the chief of staff to the First Gentleman."

"Why him?"

"Typically, the First Lady manages the Christmas tree activities. Since there's a woman in the White House, it's the responsibility of the First Gentleman. So, reaching out to his chief of staff with Christmas tree questions seemed to make sense."

"Gotcha," Lou Lou says. "I'm on board. Continue."

"I bet you take great pride in selecting the White House Christmas trees. Imagine the pride of the people and towns you choose to supply those trees. Now imagine someone were to ruin that for a town and its honor were stripped with no warning. That's how the town of Harper Hollow Falls felt when I ruined the tree destined for the White House. But guess what? They have lots of amazing, wonderful trees that you would love. I know you would, I've seen them up close . . ."

"Read it back to me," I say.

Lou Lou does.

"Perfect." I lean over her shoulder and take a screenshot with my phone.

"What are you gonna do?"

As I tap on my screen, I say to her. "I'm posting it to the White House's social media page." I stop. "Now, what to caption it?"

Lou Lou suggests, "HEY, @WHITEHOUSE, IS THIS YOUR IDEA OF A MERRY CHRISTMAS TO MAIN STREET USA?"

"Oh, that's good." I tap it out.

We stare at the screen.

When nothing happens instantly, Lou Lou says, "It might take a few minutes for the chief of staff to come up with a response for that."

"True," I say.

❄ ❄ ❄

Evening rolls around, and there's still no response from the White House.

I hear my dad roll his suitcase from his bedroom to the stairs. He sticks his head in my room and asks, "You sure you don't want to go? It's just for the night. We'd be back tomorrow for Christmas Eve."

"Dad, I haven't slept in my own bed in a month."

"OK, I thought you could help me deal with the back-woods locals."

I say, "Dad, take it easy on them. Your proposal is a lot of change for that place."

He says, "I'll keep that in mind."

❄ ❄ ❄

Tired of staring at the screen for a response for the White House, I switch to the video. *The* video, and then I toss my phone aside.

I can't stand being screenless. So I open my laptop, search for a map of Harper Hollow Falls, and see firsthand how close it is to Porter City.

Then I click on a story about the bridge that never got built. I'm reading when a window pops up with an incoming video call.

It's from Jay.

I panic. My hair!

When I don't answer, a message pops up:

PLEASE PICK UP I NEED TO TALK TO YOU.

Another call comes in.

And I answer it.

I see Jay's face, those eyes.

How could I have missed him so much in such a short period of time?

"Oh wow, you answered," he says. "Hi."

"You wanted to talk?"

"Yeah look, Mrs. Crispin came by . . ." His voice fades out a little, like he hasn't thought through what he is going to say. "Brady, I know you must think I'm a complete jerk, and I'm sure I deserve that, but—"

"I'm not angry."

"You're not?"

"I'm crushed." I repeat, "Jay, you crushed me."

"Oh. Oh man, that's so much worse. I am so, so sorry. I don't even know why I recorded it. I didn't even know you then. I was just so shocked and everything, it seemed like the thing to do, and then everyone realized that I was the only one who'd recorded it, and they were driving me crazy hitting me up for it. So I texted it, and someone posted it. I didn't mean for it to get so out of hand."

He didn't post it.

After spending time with them, I sort of understood. "I guess that makes sense." I bet Pepper posted it.

"It does?"

"Do you want me to believe you or not?"

"Yes! And I made something else . . . something to make it up to you. Your Christmas present."

He holds his phone up to the video monitor and plays a video of all the happy moments we had during my visit. There are quick clips that I didn't even notice he'd taken:

- Practicing for the ice sculpture contest
- Hot Cocoa with Mari, Pepper, and him
- Shopping
- Gingerbread houses
- Snow
- Blitzen's café and cider
- Me pulling a walleye out of the ice
- The Crispins' party

My heart tugs, and I realize that during that terrible month, I had some good times. Now it's my turn to not know what to say. "I . . . thank you. That's pretty great."

"I wanted to ask you before I post it."

I smile and nod that it's OK.

My eyes shift from the window on my laptop with Jay to the one with the bridge story.

I say, "Hey Jay, would you want to help me with something?"

CHAPTER 26

I dash through Burbank airport toting only a backpack, hoping I don't miss the red-eye. It would've been easier to go with Dad, but I didn't have this plan together when he asked me.

And how cool is my mom for helping me buy the ticket? Once I told her the whole story and what I wanted to do, she thought it was a great idea and said she was proud of me. Of course, she called the Crispins, and they agreed to look after me.

❄ ❄ ❄

When I arrive in New York in the morning, I find Jay holding a sign: BANCROFT. Seeing him fills me with a warmth that's not unlike warm sugar cookie dough. I'm so happy when his eyes light up at the sight of me.

The giant advent calendar in the terminal shows December 24.

"We have a ton of work to do," I say.

"We're ready for you."

※ ※ ※

We go straight to the tree farm. The sun isn't even up yet. With all the decorations down, and the lights and music off, the farm is dark and almost creepy.

A lone light shines from the workshop.

Jay leads the way. "Pepper and Mari started right away."

In the office, Mari breaks her focus from her laptop. "Couldn't stay away, huh?"

I say, "I don't like unfinished business."

Pepper's hair is held up by a pen. She's holding a clipboard, all business. "We have everything Jay said you needed."

I look into Mr. Schneider's office to find Mayor Winter, Kenny, and Mr. Schneider each with some sort of computer or laptop. Carmella sits next to Kenny and looks over his shoulder.

When she sees me, she rushes over to hug me. And, of course, she has warm cookies.

I say, "We have five hours before the courthouse opens."

"Your father arrived a few hours ago," Carmella says. "He's sound asleep in the Snowman Room."

I point to a giant wall map of Harper Hollow Falls that also shows Porter City and the river separating the two towns.

Mayor Winter tacks a survey of the riverbank next to the map. Then Kenny Crispin starts drawing multicolored lines over the map, carefully marking coordinates and cross-referencing with the survey.

Dan unrolls drawings of bridges and tacks them on the wall as well.

I ask, "Pepper, what have you got?"

She brings in the chalkboard that previously listed tree prices. She writes the toll averages in New York State. And then she starts writing equations in chalk.

Toll price = $1.00
Est. no. of travelers =1,000/day X 7 days/week
X 52 weeks/yr = $364,000/yr
Average operating expenses for toll bridges
within a 500-mile radius = $60,000/yr

Then Pepper says, "With interest at two percent a year, compounded annually, the bridge will pay for itself in five years."

She writes another word on the board:

Profit!

"After five years, the toll money is all profit," Kenny reiterates.

Mayor Winter says, "We just need to secure funding. If necessary, the city can take out a loan." She looks at her watch. "I'll see you at the courthouse in an hour." She picks up her coat and before she leaves, she turns around and says, "This is gonna be great. I'll see you there."

Mari and Pepper stand up and stretch.

Mari says, "I'm gonna get a quick shower. I'll meet you there."

Pepper says, "I'll catch a quick nap in your bed, and we can go over together."

Mr. Schneider yawns, picks up his keys, and makes some serious eye contact with me. In fact, I don't think he's looked me in the eye since the day of the fire, when he looked up at me and asked, "Why?" Today he says, "You're OK, Bancroft. I don't think anyone has ever done this much to help me. And, damn, it just might work."

I say, "I think it will."

I really hope it does.

CHAPTER 27

T he sun reflects off the snow and hits me right in
the face. I think that's what wakes me up . . . Wait,
wakes me up?
I fell asleep?
I look at the chair next to me, and Jay is passed out.
"We fell asleep!" I yell, and he jumps out of the chair.
He realizes right away what's happened, looks at his
watch and says, "We can make it. Let's go!"
Outside of the workshop, the ground is blanketed
with fresh snow. Even with its snow tires, there's no way
the golf cart will make it to the courthouse.
I ask, "How are we gonna get there?"
"I know a way." And Jay runs out the door.

❄ ❄ ❄

It's bitterly cold and still snowing. I look to my right up the street, and then left.

Where is he?

Before I see him, I hear something. Dogs barking. Then, flying through the drifts, there is Jay, and he's . . . I don't actually believe it . . . he's in a sleigh being pulled by six huskies.

He tugs back on their reins, and I get on behind him.

"You're gonna need this." He hands me the stocking cap Carmella gave to me on our first day.

"Mush!" he calls, and the dogs excitedly pull us toward the courthouse.

I wrap my hands around his waist so I don't fall off the back. "Do I want to ask where you got this?"

"Mrs. Kimball, up the street. This is how she picks up her tree every year."

"Well, OK. Next year she gets a discount," I say.

"Everyone gets a discount!" he shouts into the wind.

I hold on for my life, that stocking cap blowing behind us in the wind. My face is freezing, so I bury it in Jay's back. We fly past Lily in her cruiser, and she follows us with sirens bleeping.

The dogsled careens into a snowbank. We bound off it and sprint to the courthouse. "What about the dogs?" I yell to Jay.

"They know their way home!"

I can see Lily's cruiser skid to a stop; she gets out and chases us, but we don't have time to stop and explain.

We take the steps of the courthouse two at a time. The door slams when I push it open.

My dad and several men in black suits huddle around the table in front of the fireplace that I sat at when I testified at my hearing.

I announce, "Stop! You're making a big mistake!"

My dad turns around. "Brady?"

Then my dad's boss, a grouchy, gray-haired guy with the physique of a Twizzler, says to my dad, "Rob, what's the meaning of this?"

Lily finally catches up. She's winded. "I've got it under control. You two are under arrest for—"

From behind the wall of men in suits comes a voice through a megaphone. "Put down the handcuffs."

The suits spread, showing Mayor Winter behind the table in a fluffy Christmas bathrobe.

Into the megaphone, she says, "No one is getting arrested." She puts the megaphone down. "Go ahead, Brady."

"Dad, I need to talk to all of you. Right now."

Pepper opens her laptop to our presentation.

"Gentleman, look around," I say.

They do.

"I mean, look down and around. At everyone's feet."

They do.

"No one wears sneakers here. Sneakers don't work in the snow. They only have summer for a few weeks in this town. What they need is a bridge. What they need even more than a bridge is a profitable bridge." I point to the laptop. "Let me run you through the numbers."

I go through the whole presentation.

When I'm done, Twizzler whispers in Dad's ear. I wonder if Dad has just gotten fired. But when Twizzler also whispers in the ears of the other suits, I figure he hasn't fired all of them.

Twizzler nods to my dad.

Dad says, "Your honor, we'd like to withdraw our bid to buy the tree farm. Instead, we want to be majority investors in the Harper Hollow Falls bridge to Porter City, Canada."

Mayor Winter bangs her gavel. "Granted. Court adjourned. Now get out of here and celebrate Christmas Eve."

Jay hugs me!

Pepper and Mari high-five me.

Carmella and Kenny can't stop clapping.

Mr. Schneider calls, "Cider is on me!"

CHAPTER 28

*T*he Crispins and I trudge through the snow to Harper Hollow Falls' annual Christmas Eve gathering in the town square. Sturdy Stan McSpruce's lights and glass decorations twinkle brightly in the freshly fallen snow. I open my mouth and catch a rogue snowflake on my tongue.

Mmmm.

The carolers in hooded velvet cloaks have ramped up their pep levels since the Crispins' party. They're nailing every verse of "We Wish You a Merry Christmas."

The podium, the same one Mayor Winter stood at for the goodbye ceremony, now sports a glittery CHRISTMAS EVE sign, and decorated trees sit on either side.

Mayor Winter, who's swapped her bathrobe for a full-length red dress edged with white faux fur, puts on her ceremonial top hat and takes the podium. Through her megaphone, she joins the carolers in "Jingle Bells"—she's horrible!—and everyone follows her lead. At "*one horse open sleigh* . . . ," she signals them to cut.

Mayor Winter doesn't make a joke as part of her opening monologue. Instead, she's serious, "Friends, I have a confession."

This seems very unlike her. I scan the crowd, and every eye is on the mayor, awaiting this confession. I see my dad. I'm shocked at who I see with him: Mom.

She's here too!

And both of them are wearing stocking caps à la Carmella.

The mayor continues. "I never believed that Brady Bancroft ruined Christmas."

There's grumbling, confusion . . .

"But I don't think this was an accident, either. What I mean is that things happen for a reason, and I think that what happened with the White House Christmas tree was a blessing in disguise"—more groans from the towns-people—"because it reminded us what really matters to Harper Hollow Falls. You see, we needed her as much as she needed us."

The Mayor's speech is interrupted by a black SUV with tinted windows and government tags.

Its door opens, and a man in a dark suit and sun-glasses gets out and makes his way to the podium.

Lily intercepts him.

They exchange words. He flashes a badge. Then Lily escorts him to Mayor Winter and whispers something in her ear.

The mayor steps aside.

The man puts the megaphone to his mouth. "Would Mr. Daniel Schneider please come forward?"

Mr. Schneider takes off his red ball cap.

The crowd divides to make room for him to get to the podium.

The government man hands Mr. Schneider a letter. I can make out the White House logo from a distance. He takes a moment to read it.

Mr. Schneider doesn't use a megaphone to explain to the crowd, "It's from the White House." He wipes a tear from his eye. "They're paying for next year's tree in advance." He waves a check over his head. "It's enough to cover the taxes."

The crowd cheers!

The government man says into the megaphone, "And the First Gentleman heard about your gingerbread houses. He'd like one for every room in the White House."

Mrs. Crispin gasps and hugs me.

Jay whispers to me, "Looks like you have your work cut out for you."

"Mrs. Crispin has been my mentor. I'm sure she's up to the challenge."

＊　＊　＊

I go with Mom and Dad to retrieve Dad's bag from the Yuletide.

Carmella has made us a fabulous bag of cookies to take home. She asks, "Are you sure you won't stay?"

Mom says, "We've never been away from home at Christmas."

I glance at my phone and say, "Oh, drat! It looks like the airport is closed due to snow."

Dad peeks over my shoulder to see the breaking news, but I pull it away. We exchange a quick glance, and he knows what I'm doing.

Dad says, "I hear Christmas is a pretty big deal here . . ."

Mom adds, "We'd love to stay."

CHAPTER 29

Christmas Day

Kenny Crispin carries a steaming golden turkey to the dining room table and puts it right in front of me.

Around the table are all the people I love: Mom, Dad, Jay, Pepper, Mari, Mr. Schneider, Mayor Winter, Kenny, Carmella, and Lily. Lily has brought her new boyfriend, Jamaal. Lou Lou, who would never miss a Bancroft Christmas dinner, is on Facetime.

Carmella says to me, "Brady, we'd like you to do the honors of carving."

Kenny hands me his carving knife and takes his seat at the head of the table.

Uh . . . I've never carved a turkey before.

I ask the person next to me, "Mr. Schneider, will you help me?"

He takes the knife. "Of course, Brady."

He's really good at it, and soon everyone's plate is full, and the room is filled with merriment.

Kenny asks my dad, "So how are you going to manage all this bridge business?"

My mom inhales like she's going to speak for him, like she always does, but my dad puts his hand on hers. He's got this.

"Well, Ken, a bridge is a big deal. And it needs daily attention. I think someone needs to be here to oversee things."

Mom says, "That's a far commute, Rob."

I say, "Mom, I think he wants us to move here . . . to live here."

Dad asks me and Mom, "If that's all right?"

Mom looks around the table. "I'd like to be part of this community."

I say, "It's exactly what I want for Christmas."

Then I look at Lou Lou on the phone. She's dabbing tears. She says, "Get a house with an extra bedroom for me. I'll visit every few weeks."

❅ ❅ ❅

The celebration continues after dinner. Music plays and gifts are exchanged.

At last, it's a good time to give presents to Jay, Pepper, and Mari.

I bring them over to the tree.

Mari opens hers first. "The gloves! How did you remember with everything else that is going on?"

I say, "It's easy to remember when it's important."

And Mari hugs me.

Then Pepper opens her planner. "First thing that's going in here is a production schedule for next year's gingerbread houses."

Lastly, Jay opens his. It's the key fob/finder that he admired. "I can't believe it! I need this so badly."

I say, "I hope you like it."

Jay says, "Best. Christmas. Ever." And he puts his arm around me.

I take my camera out to get a selfie of the four of us.

My camera flash goes off, causing a moment of blindness.

And that's immediately followed by the unmistakable sound of the Crispins' Christmas tree falling to the ground.

The End

ABOUT THE AUTHOR

*C*indy Callaghan is the award-winning author of the mega-popular *Just Add Magic* and *Just Add Magic 2: Potion Problems*, five *Lost in* books: *London, Ireland, Paris, Rome*, and *Hollywood*, and two stand-alones: the award-winning *Sydney Mackenzie Knocks 'Em Dead* and *Saltwater Secrets*.

Just Add Magic has been developed into an Emmy-nominated Amazon Original live-action series in its fifth season and is now being distributed worldwide via Nickelodeon. Her most recent book, *Saltwater Secrets,* is set up at a major studio.

The Girl Who Ruined Christmas is her tenth novel. In addition to writing, Cindy's passions include animal advocacy, running, movie-going, reading, podcasts, and friends, all of which take a backseat to her three children, husband, and menagerie of rescued-pets.

Author photo © Lighteous Photography

SELECTED TITLES FROM SPARKPRESS

SparkPress is an independent boutique publisher delivering high-quality, entertaining, and engaging content that enhances readers' lives, with a special focus on female-driven work: www.gosparkpress.com.

The Leaving Year:A Novel, Pam McGaffin. $16.95, 978-1-943006-81-6. As the Summer of Love comes to an end, 15-year-old Ida Petrovich waits for a father who never comes home. While commercial fishing in Alaska, he is lost at sea, but with no body and no wreckage, Ida and her mother are forced to accept a "presumed" death that tests their already strained relationship. While still in shock over the loss of her father, Ida overhears an adult conversation that shatters everything she thought she knew about him. This prompts her to set out on a search for the truth that takes her from her Washington State hometown to Southeast Alaska.

A Song for the Road: A Novel, Rayne Lacko. $16.95, 978-1-684630-02-8. When his house is destroyed by a tornado, fifteen-year-old Carter Danforth steals his mom's secret cash stash, buys his father's guitar back from a pawnshop, and hitchhikes old Route 66 in search of the man who left him as a child.

Tree Dreams:A Novel, Kristin Kaye. $16.95, 978-1-943006-46-5. In the often-violent battle between loggers and environmentalists that plagues seventeen-year-old Jade's hometown in Northern California, she must decide whose side she's on—but choosing sides only makes matters worse.